# Zinc ALLOY

## REVEALED!

**Librarian Reviewer**
Julie Potvin Kirchner
Educator, Wayzata Public Schools
MA in Education, The College of Saint Catherine, Saint Paul, MN
MLS, Texas Woman's University

**Reading Consultant**
Elizabeth Stedem
Educator/Consultant, Colorado Springs, CO
MA in Elementary Education, University of Denver, CO

STONE ARCH BOOKS
www.stonearchbooks.com

Graphic Sparks are published by Stone Arch Books
151 Good Counsel Drive, P.O. Box 669
Mankato, Minnesota 56002
*www.stonearchbooks.com*

*Library of Congress Cataloging-in-Publication Data*
Lemke, Donald.
    Revealed! / by Donald Lemke; illustrated by Douglas Holgate.
    p. cm. — (Graphic Sparks. Zinc Alloy)
    ISBN 978-1-4342-0763-0 (library binding)
    ISBN 978-1-4342-0859-0 (pbk.)
    1. Graphic novels. [1. Graphic novels. 2. Heroes—Fiction. 3. Robots—Fiction.
4. Bullies—Fiction.] I. Holgate, Douglas, ill. II. Title.
PZ7.7.L33Re 2009
[Fic]—dc22                                        2008006711

Summary: When Zack Allen reveals his secret superhero identity, everything in his life
changes. Suddenly, he's the coolest kid at school and the world's greatest athlete. But can
he compete without wearing the Zinc Alloy suit? Find out what happens when the robot
suit comes off.

Art Director: Heather Kindseth
Graphic Designer: Brann Garvey

1 2 3 4 5 6 13 12 11 10 09 08

Printed in the United States of America

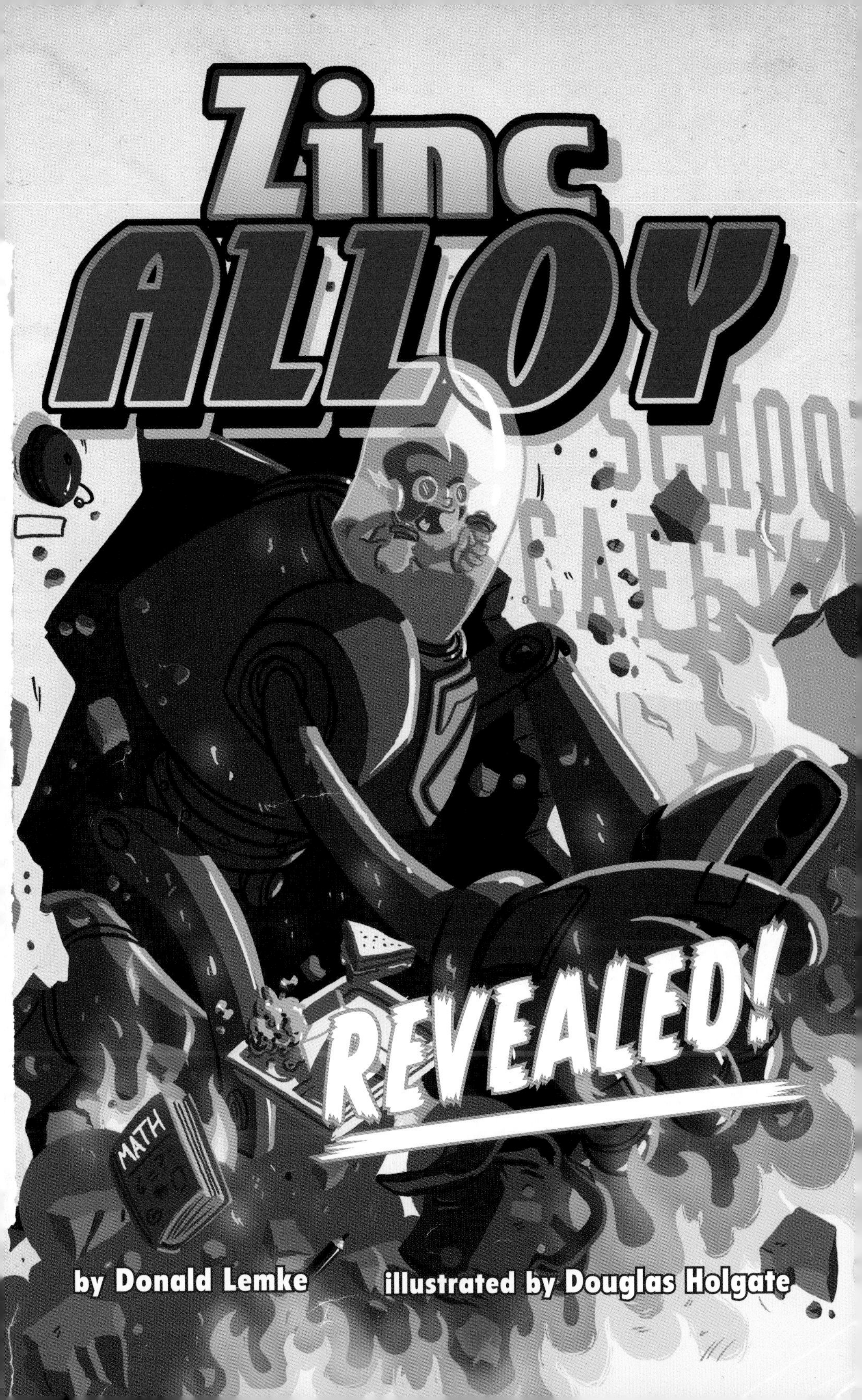
Zinc Alloy
REVEALED!
MATH
by Donald Lemke
illustrated by Douglas Holgate

# Cast of Characters

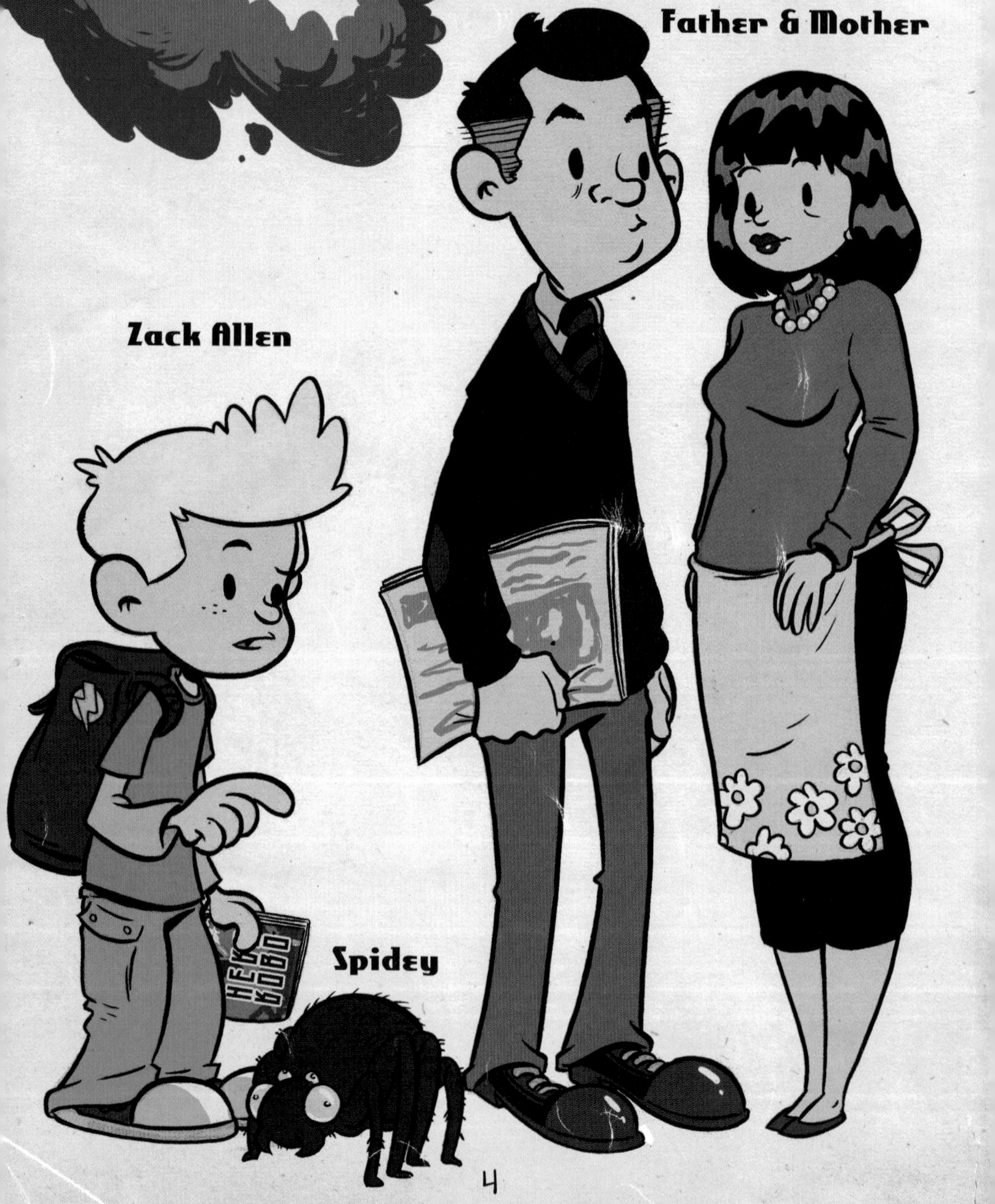
Father & Mother
Zack Allen
Spidey
HEX ROBO

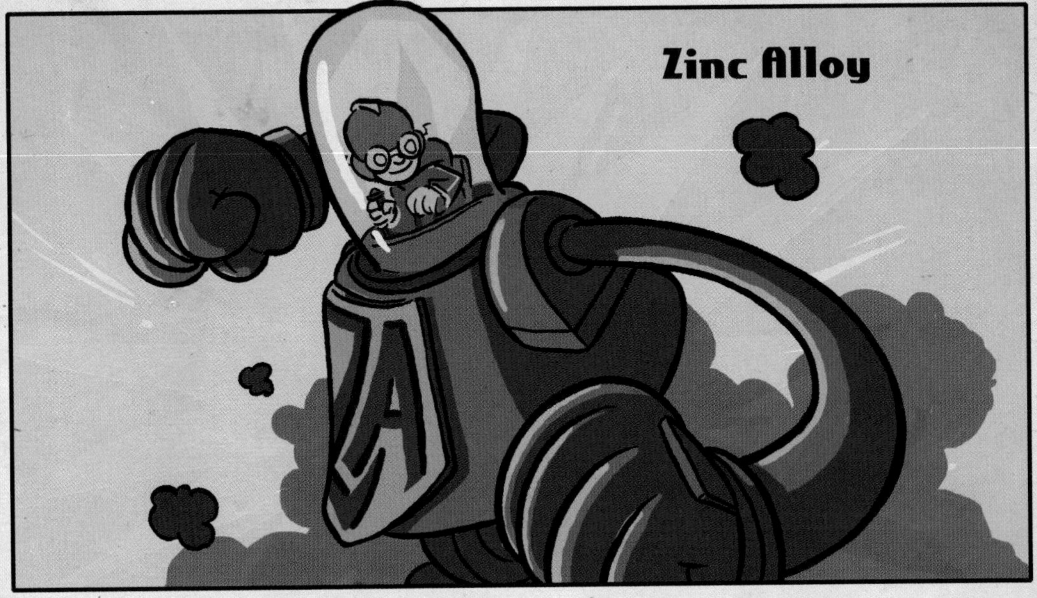
Zinc Alloy

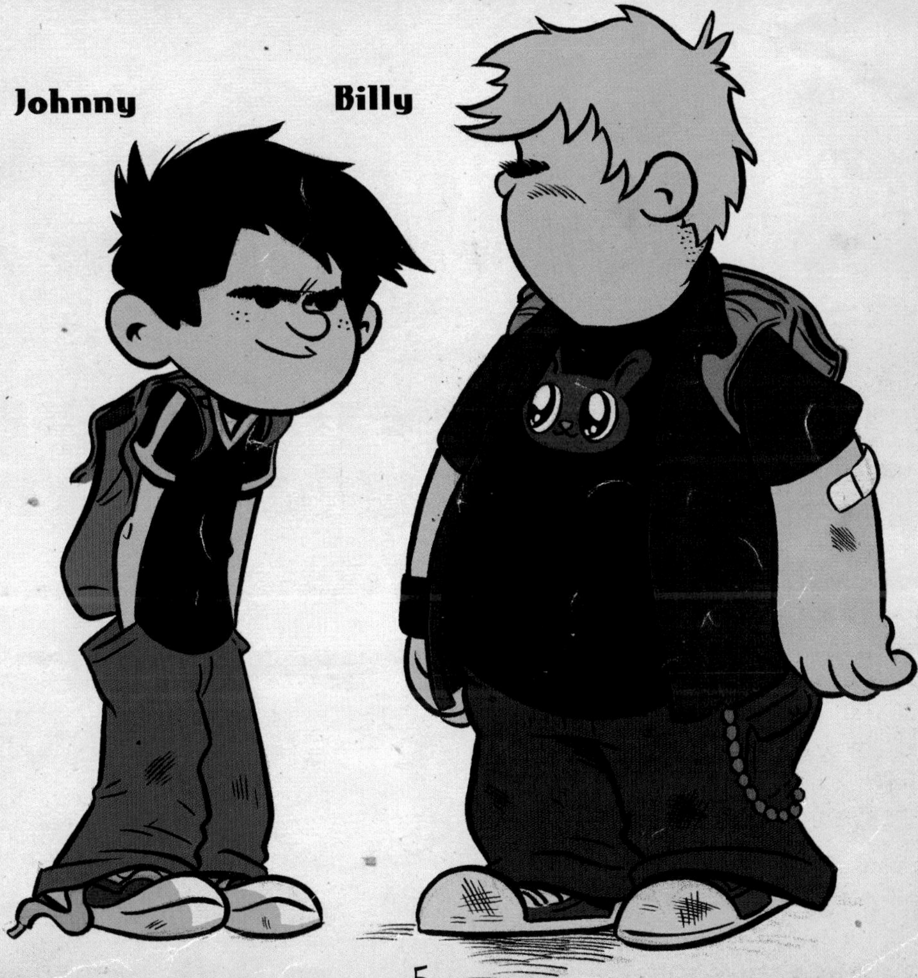
Johnny
Billy

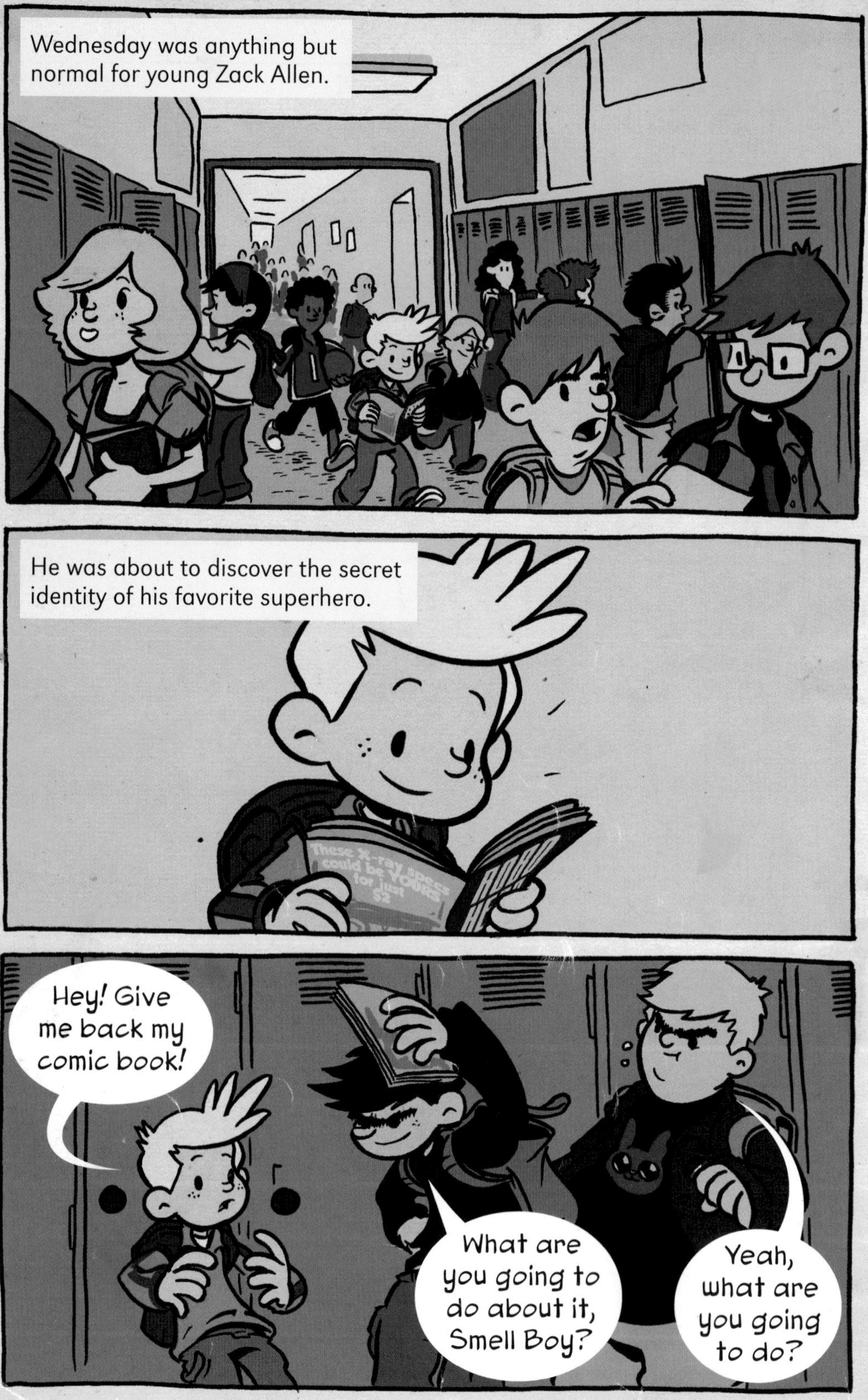
Wednesday was anything but normal for young Zack Allen.
He was about to discover the secret identity of his favorite superhero.
These X-ray specs could be YOURS for just $2
Hey! Give me back my comic book!
What are you going to do about it, Smell Boy?
Yeah, what are you going to do?

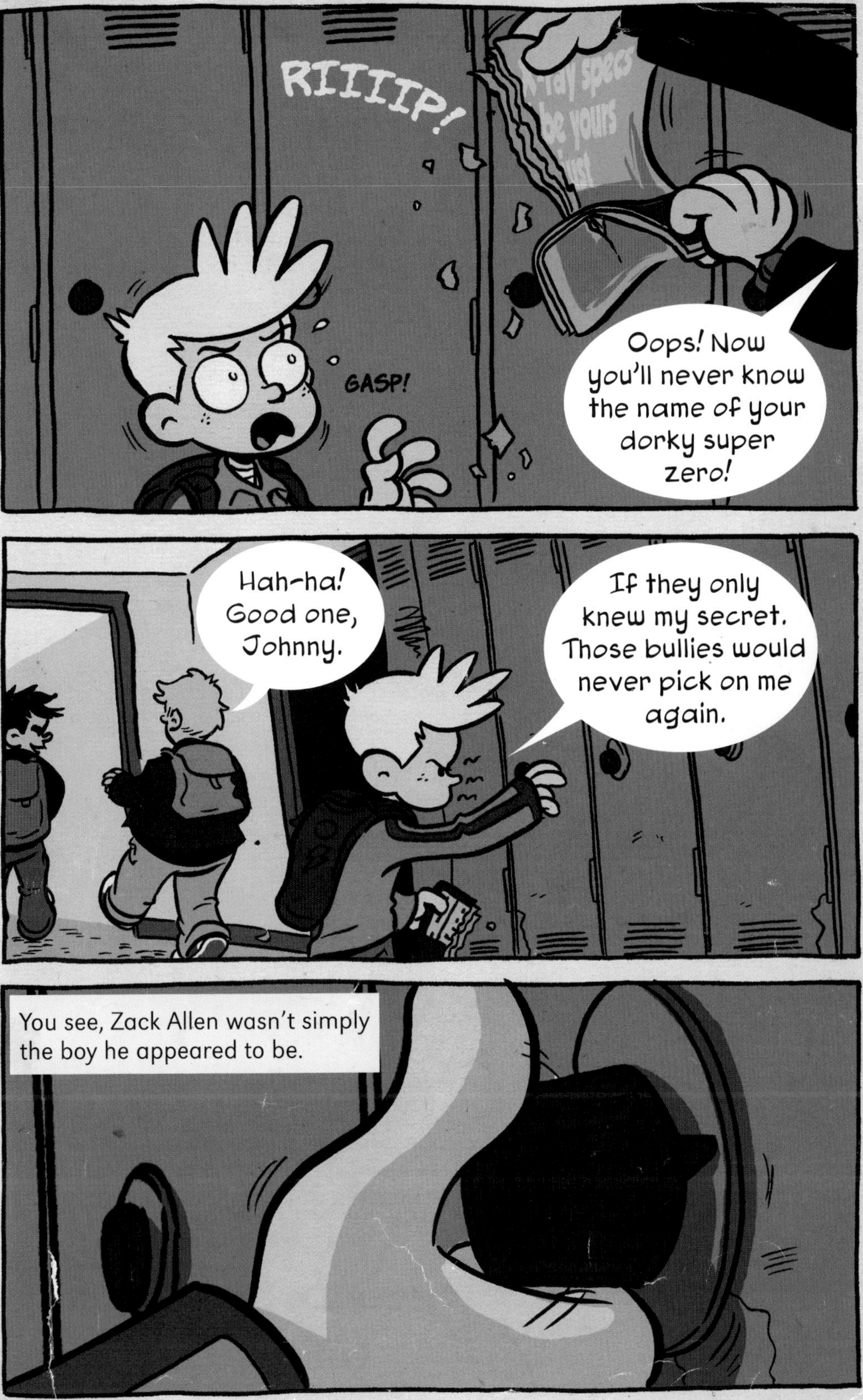
RIIIIP!
GASP!
Oops! Now you'll never know the name of your dorky super zero!
Hah-ha! Good one, Johnny.
If they only knew my secret. Those bullies would never pick on me again.
You see, Zack Allen wasn't simply the boy he appeared to be.

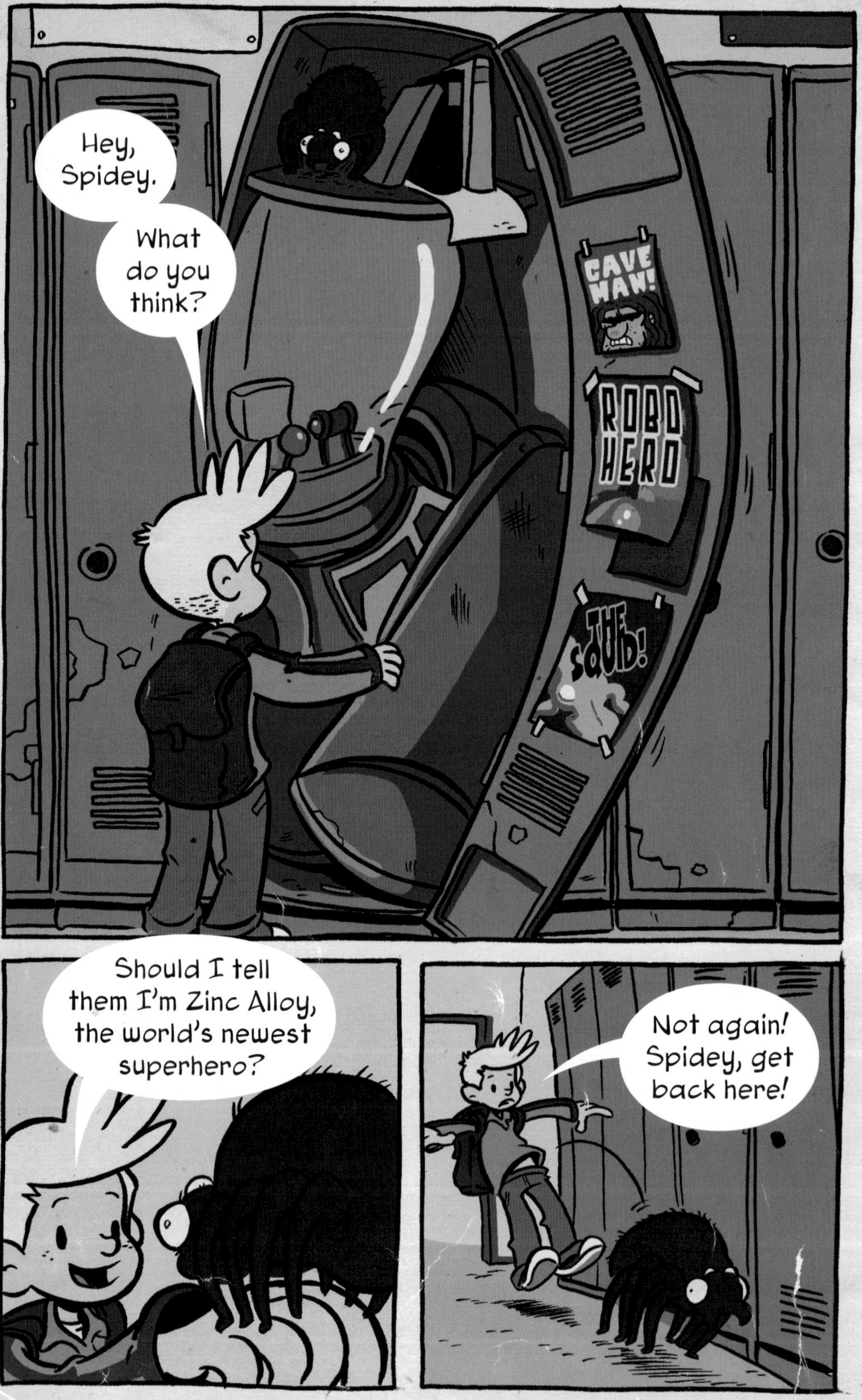
Hey, Spidey.
What do you think?
CAVE MAN!
ROBO HERO
THE SQUID!
Should I tell them I'm Zinc Alloy, the world's newest superhero?
Not again! Spidey, get back here!

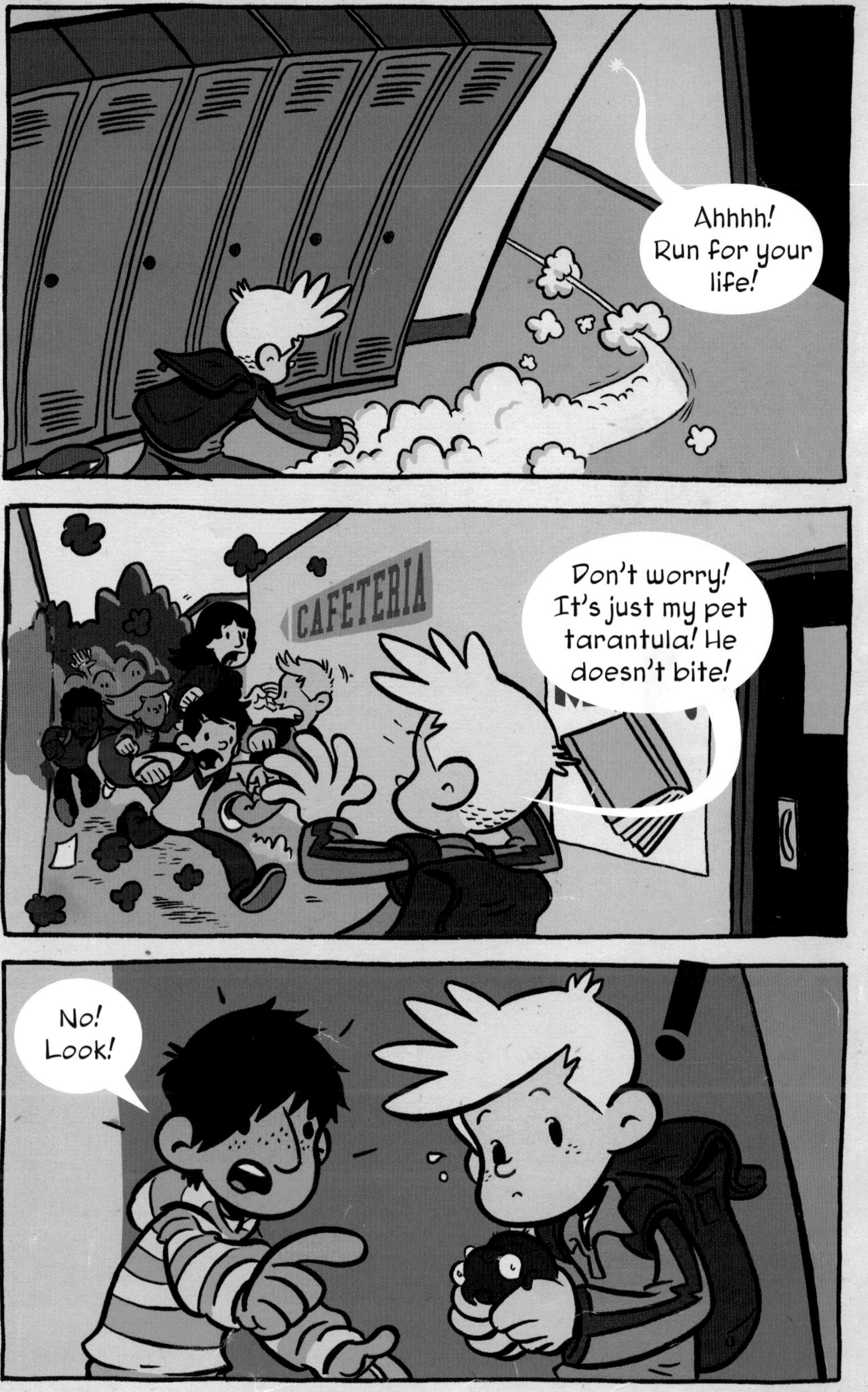
Ahhhh! Run for your life!
CAFETERIA
Don't worry! It's just my pet tarantula! He doesn't bite!
No! Look!

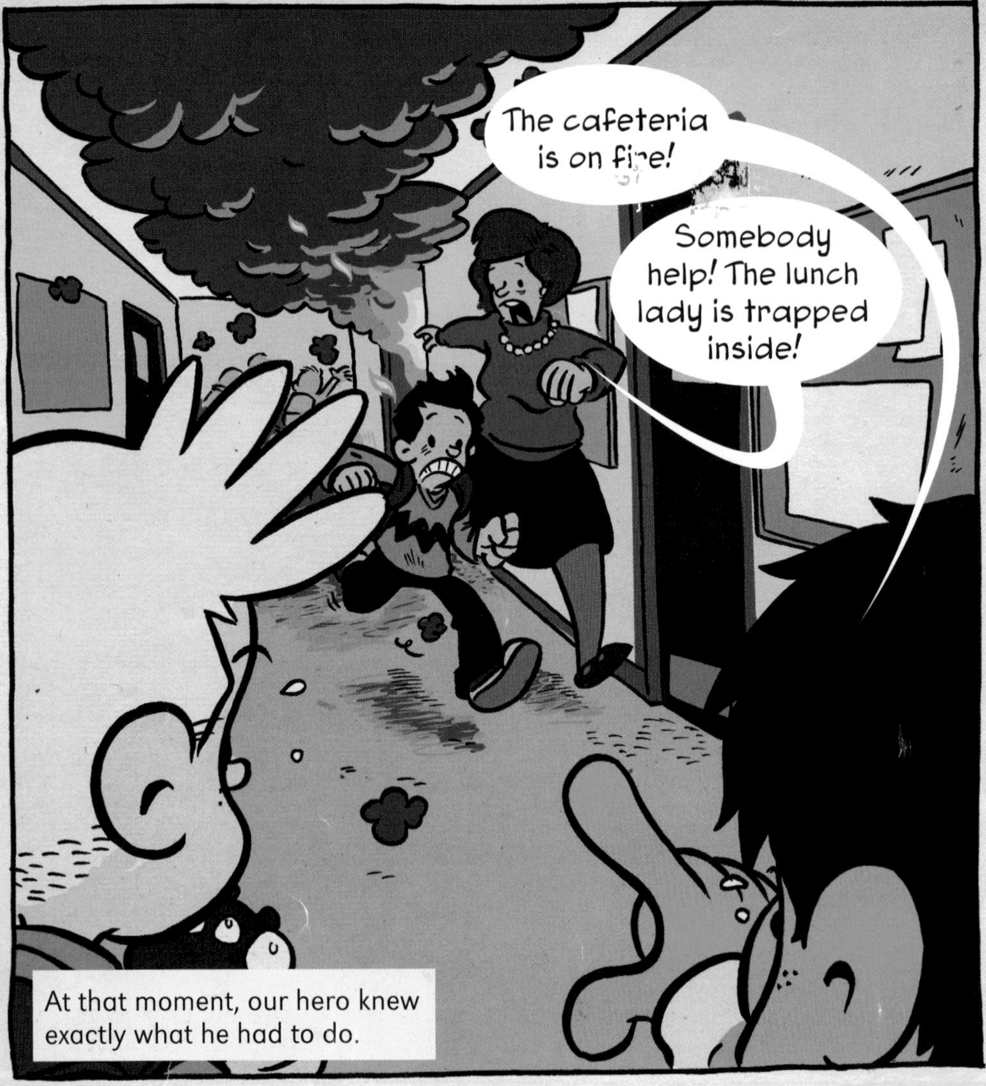
The cafeteria is on fire!
Somebody help! The lunch lady is trapped inside!
At that moment, our hero knew exactly what he had to do.

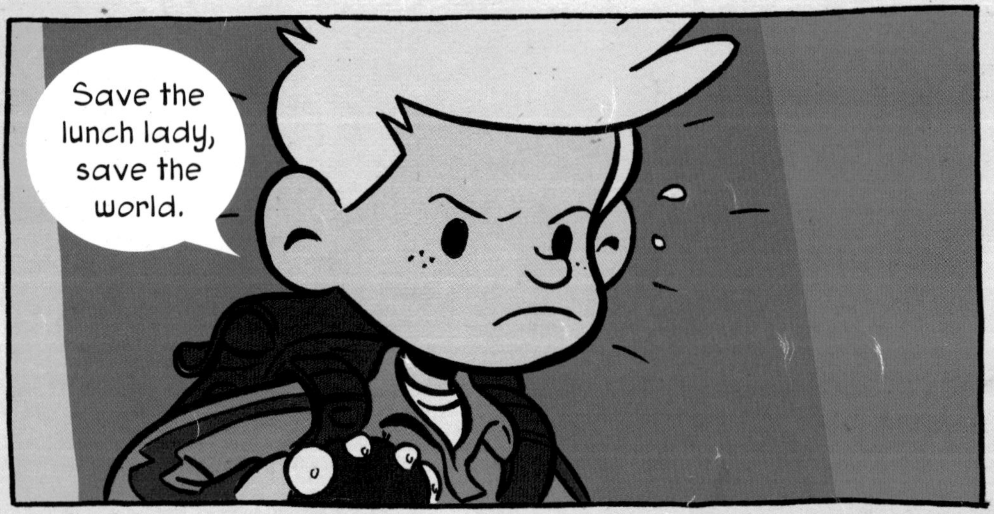
Save the lunch lady, save the world.

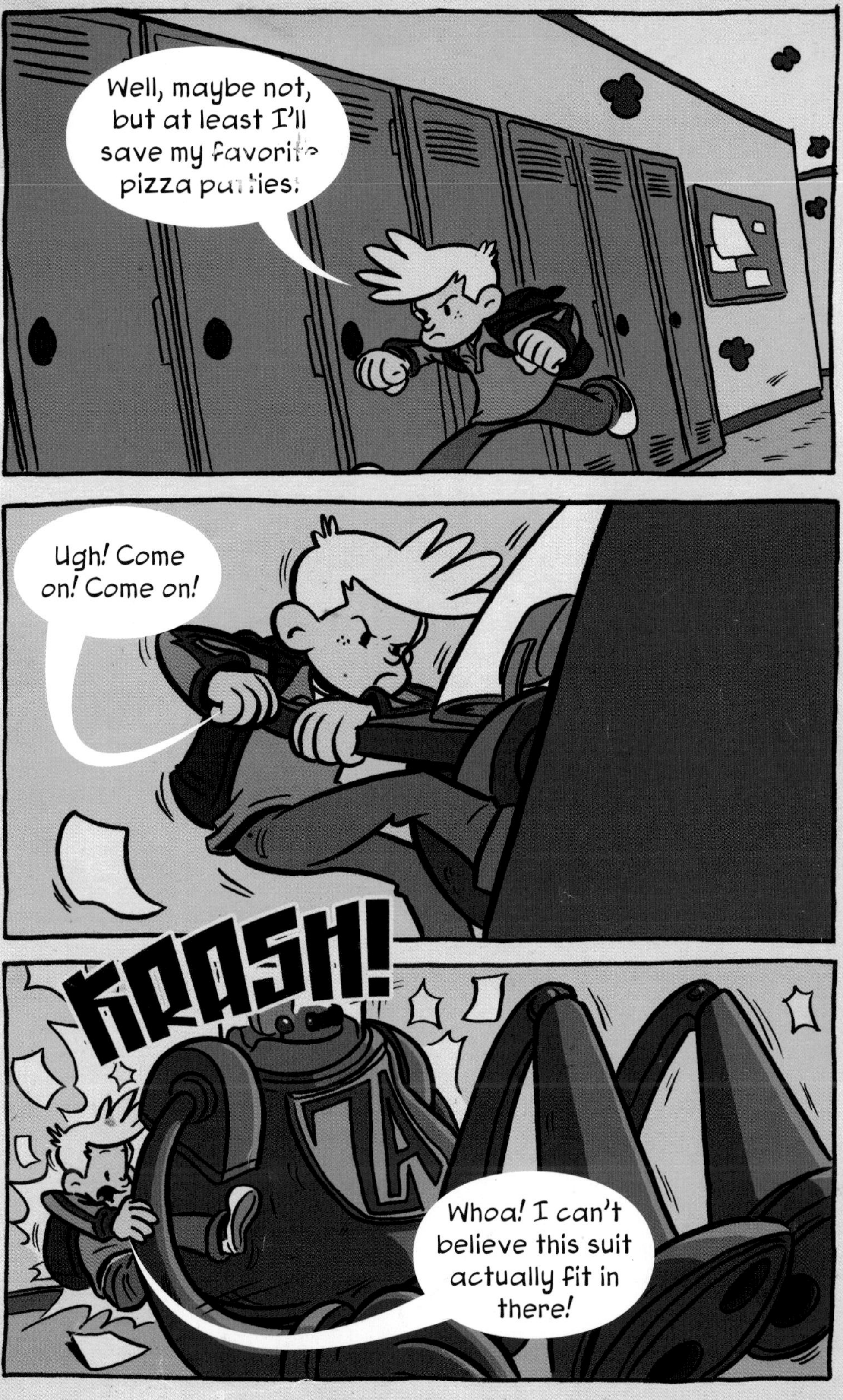
Well, maybe not, but at least I'll save my favorite pizza parties!
Ugh! Come on! Come on!
KRASH!
Whoa! I can't believe this suit actually fit in there!

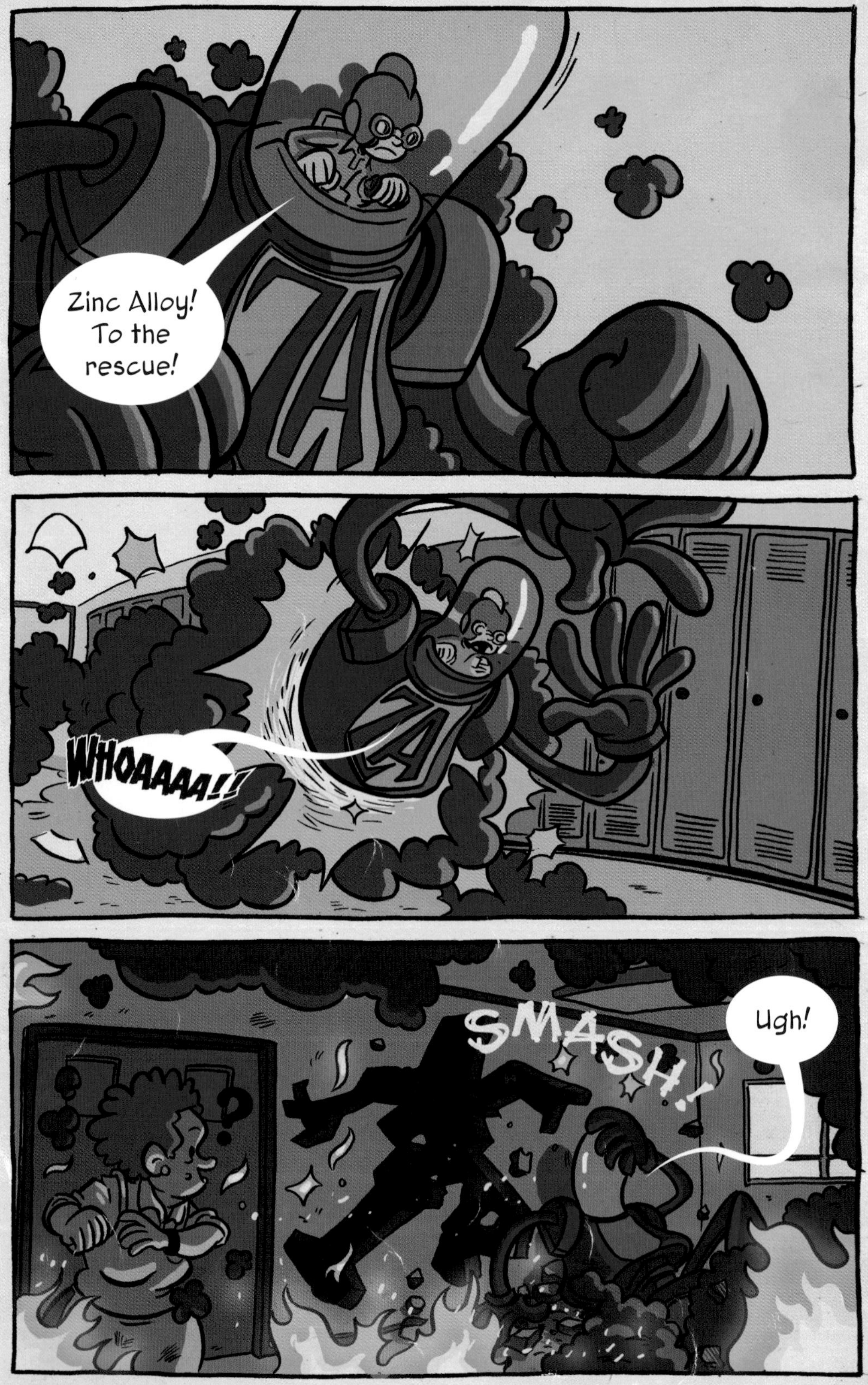
Zinc Alloy! To the rescue!
WHOAAAA!!
SMASH!
Ugh!

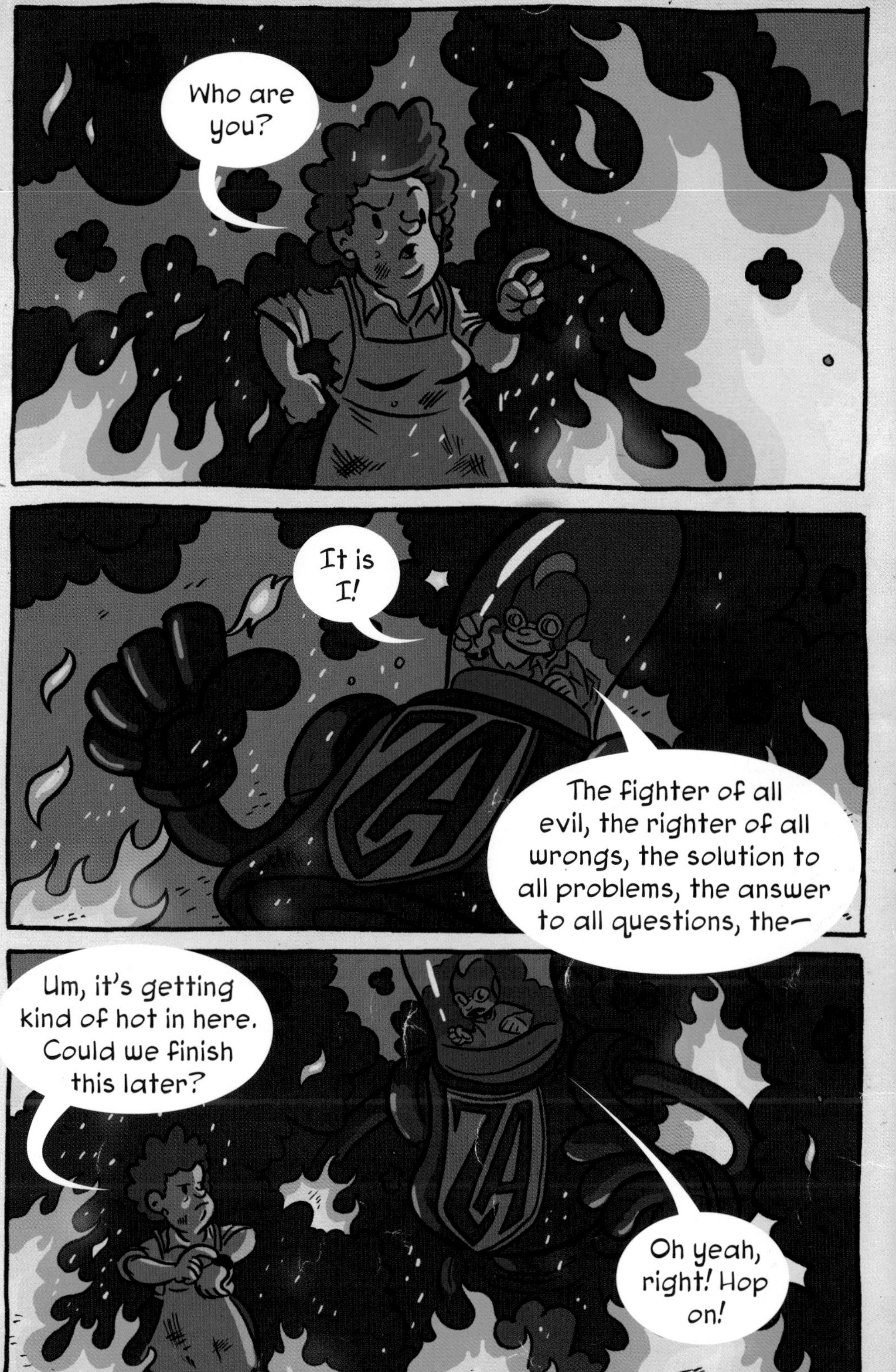
Who are you?
It is I!
The fighter of all evil, the righter of all wrongs, the solution to all problems, the answer to all questions, the—
Um, it's getting kind of hot in here. Could we finish this later?
Oh yeah, right! Hop on!

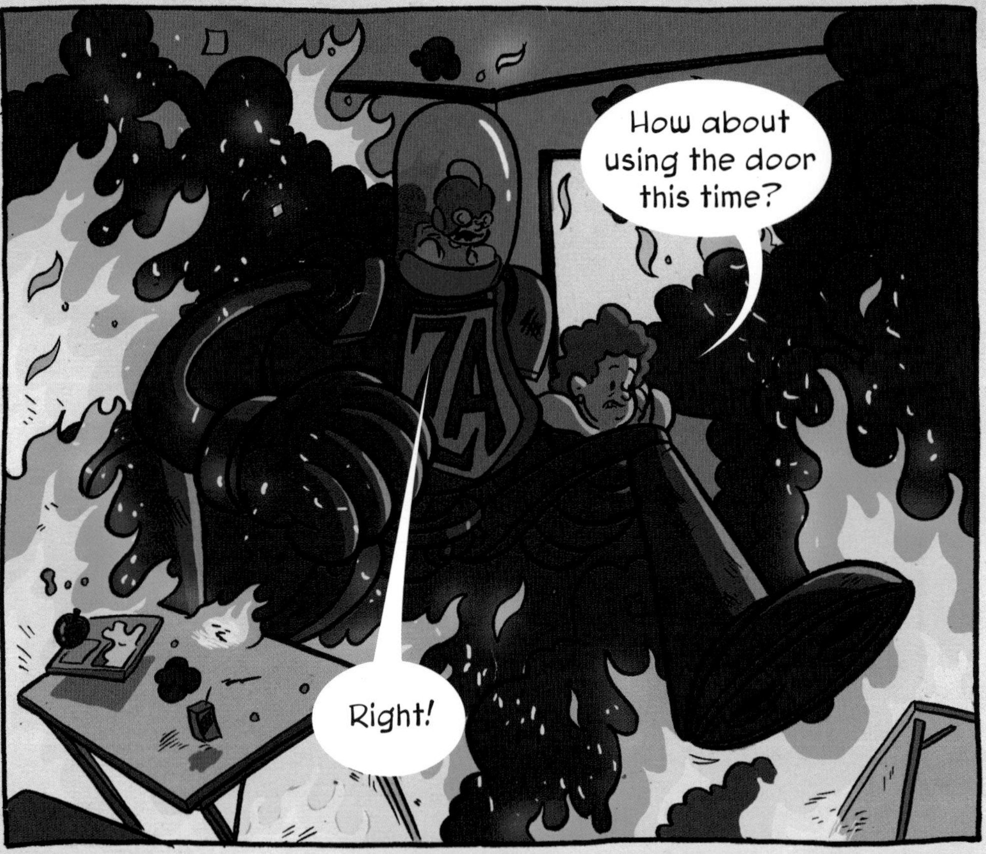
How about using the door this time?
Right!

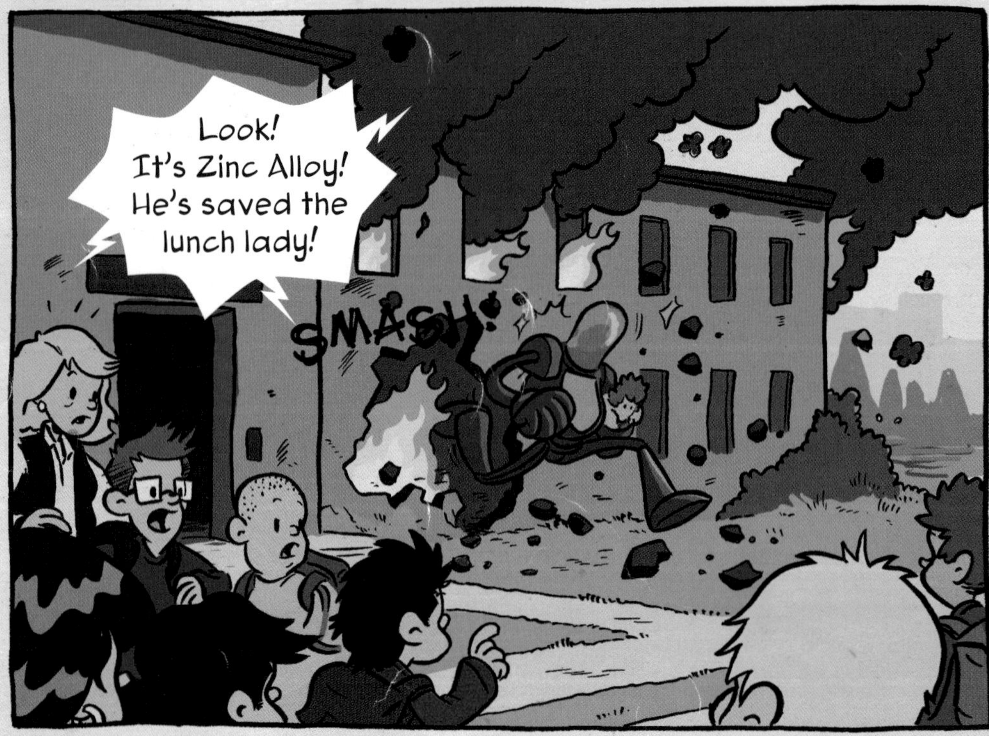
Look! It's Zinc Alloy! He's saved the lunch lady!
SMASH!

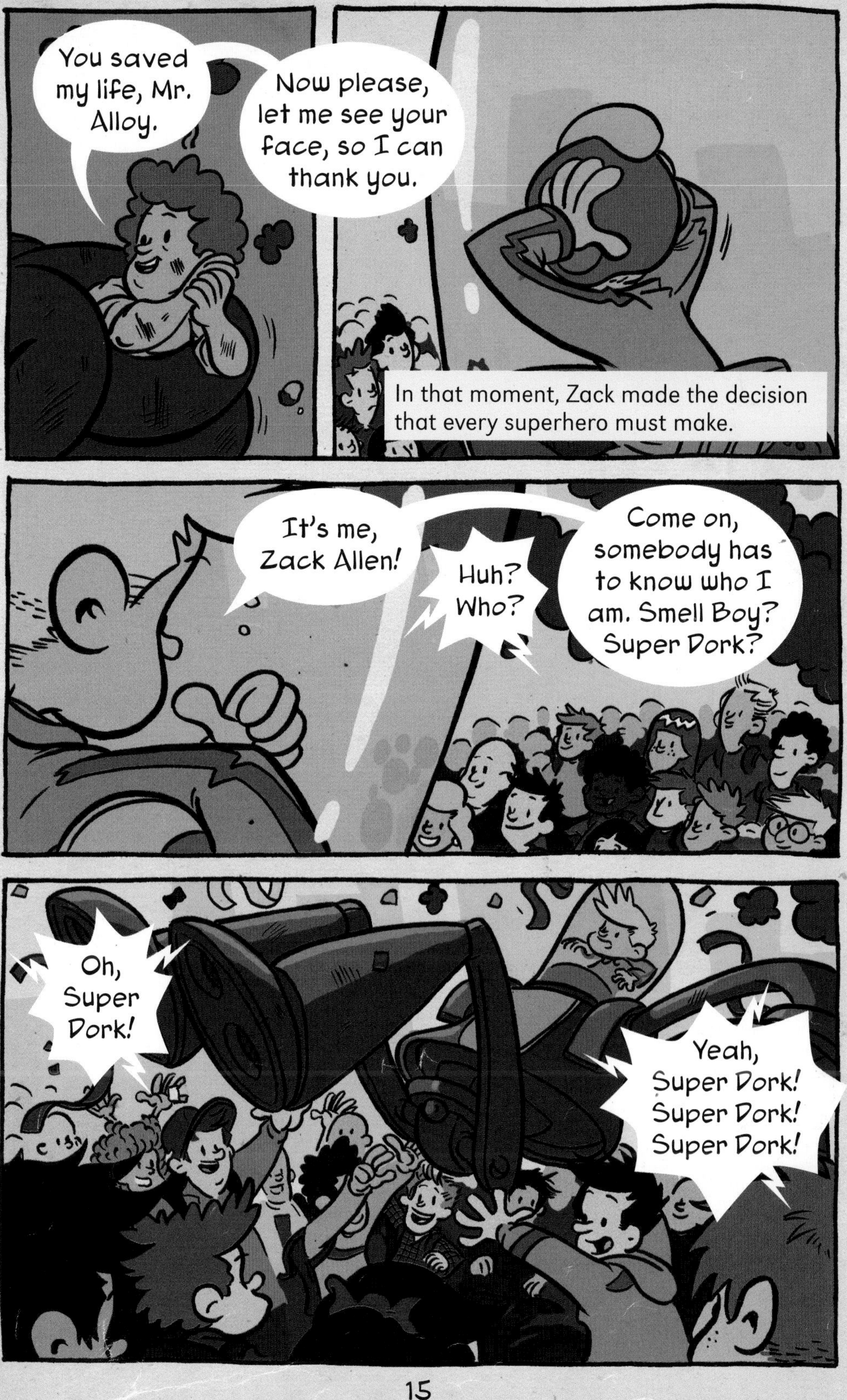

You saved my life, Mr. Alloy.
Now please, let me see your face, so I can thank you.
In that moment, Zack made the decision that every superhero must make.
It's me, Zack Allen!
Huh? Who?
Come on, somebody has to know who I am. Smell Boy? Super Dork?
Oh, Super Dork!
Yeah, Super Dork! Super Dork! Super Dork!

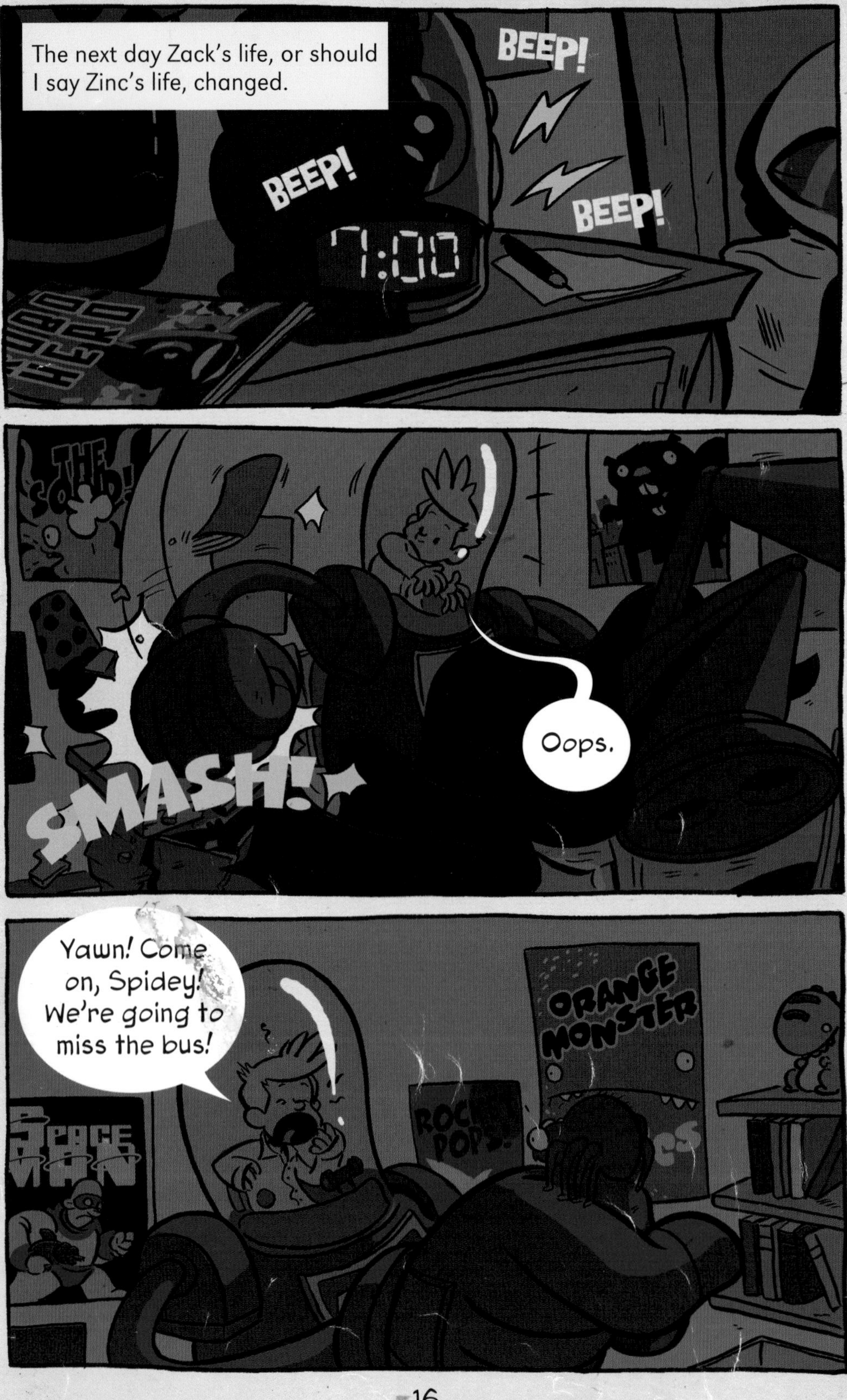
The next day Zack's life, or should I say Zinc's life, changed.
BEEP!
BEEP!
BEEP!
7:00
SMASH!
Oops.
Yawn! Come on, Spidey! We're going to miss the bus!
ORANGE MONSTER

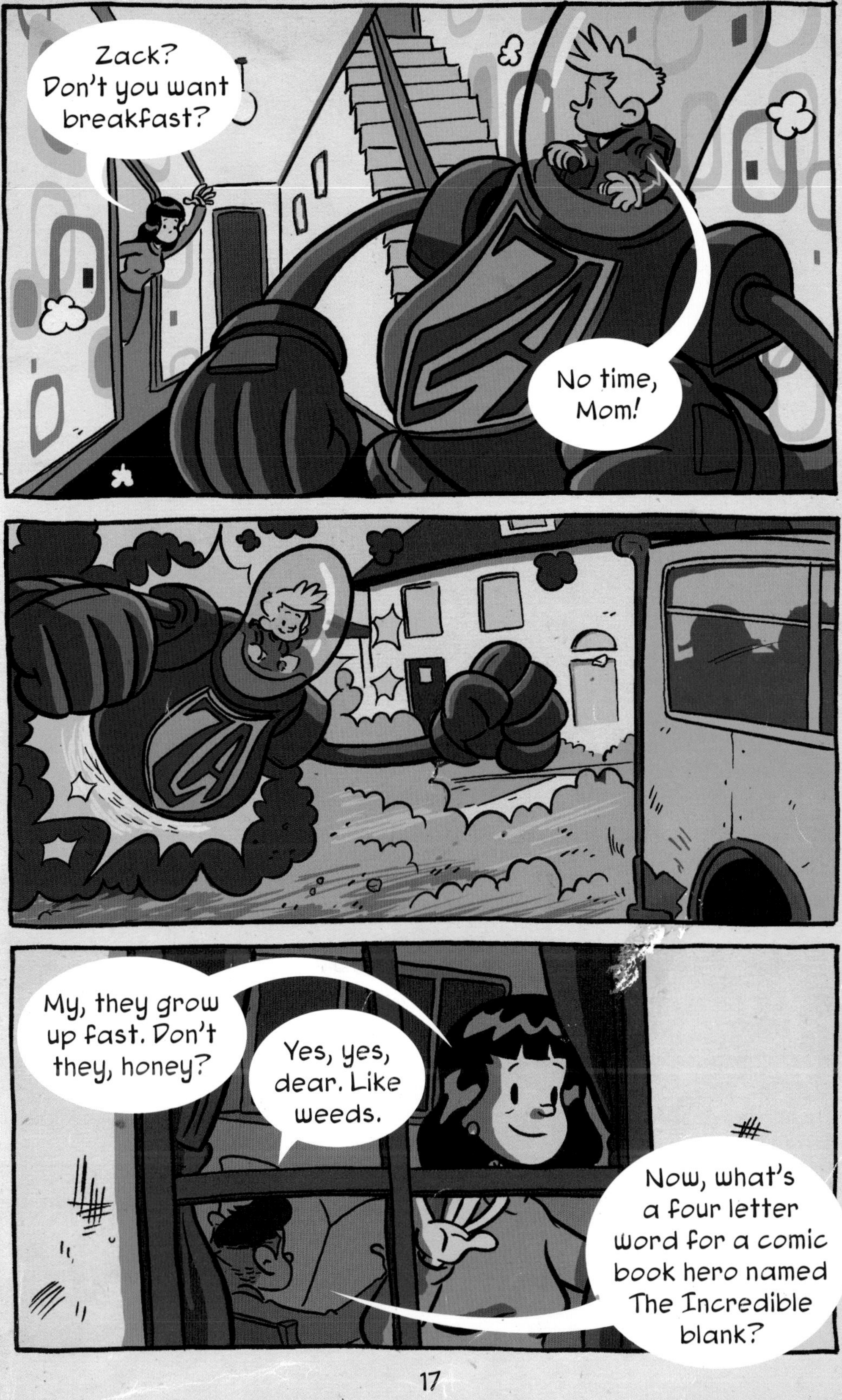
Zack? Don't you want breakfast?
No time, Mom!
My, they grow up fast. Don't they, honey?
Yes, yes, dear. Like weeds.
Now, what's a four letter word for a comic book hero named The Incredible blank?

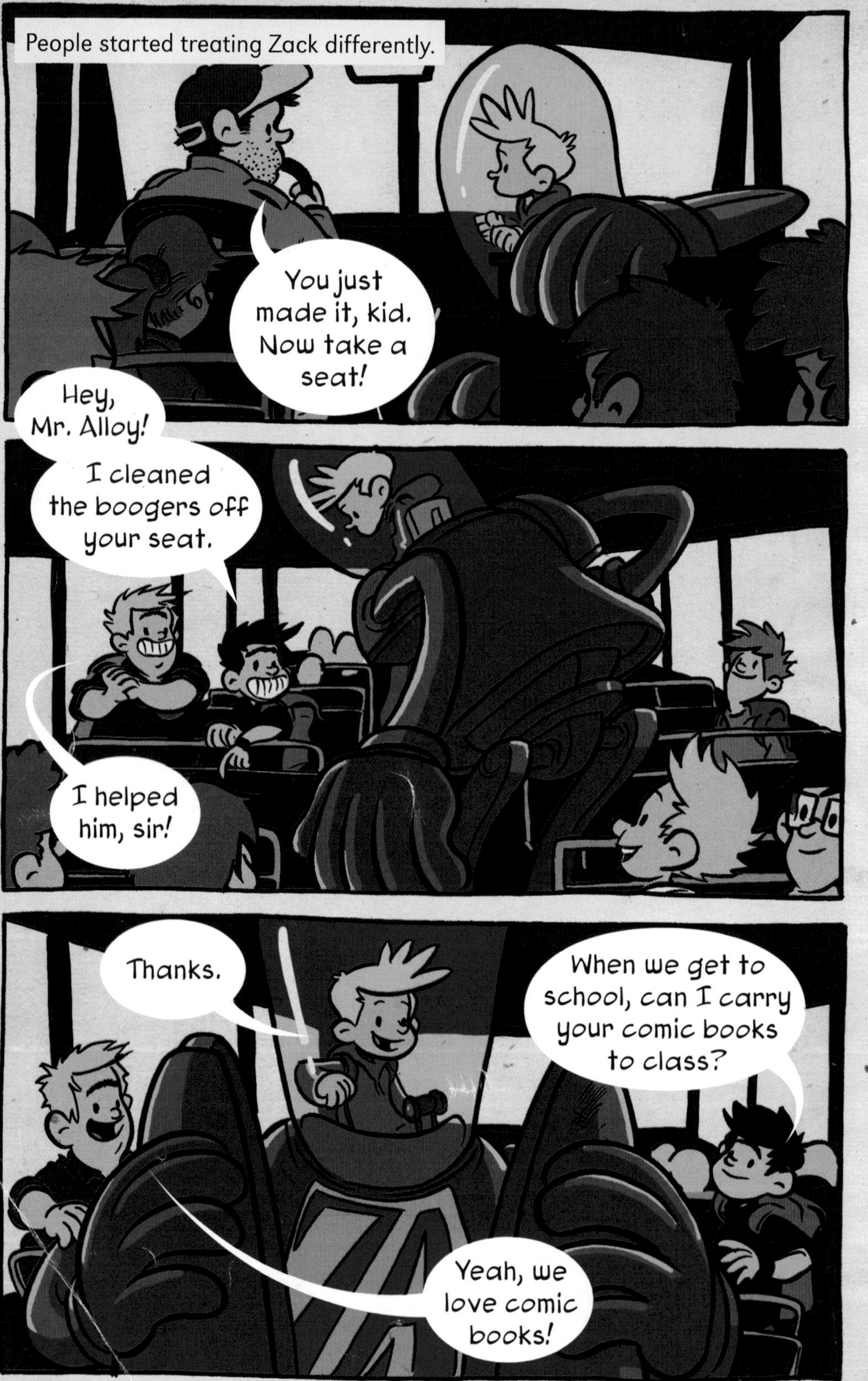
People started treating Zack differently.
You just made it, kid. Now take a seat!
Hey, Mr. Alloy!
I cleaned the boogers off your seat.
I helped him, sir!
Thanks.
When we get to school, can I carry your comic books to class?
Yeah, we love comic books!

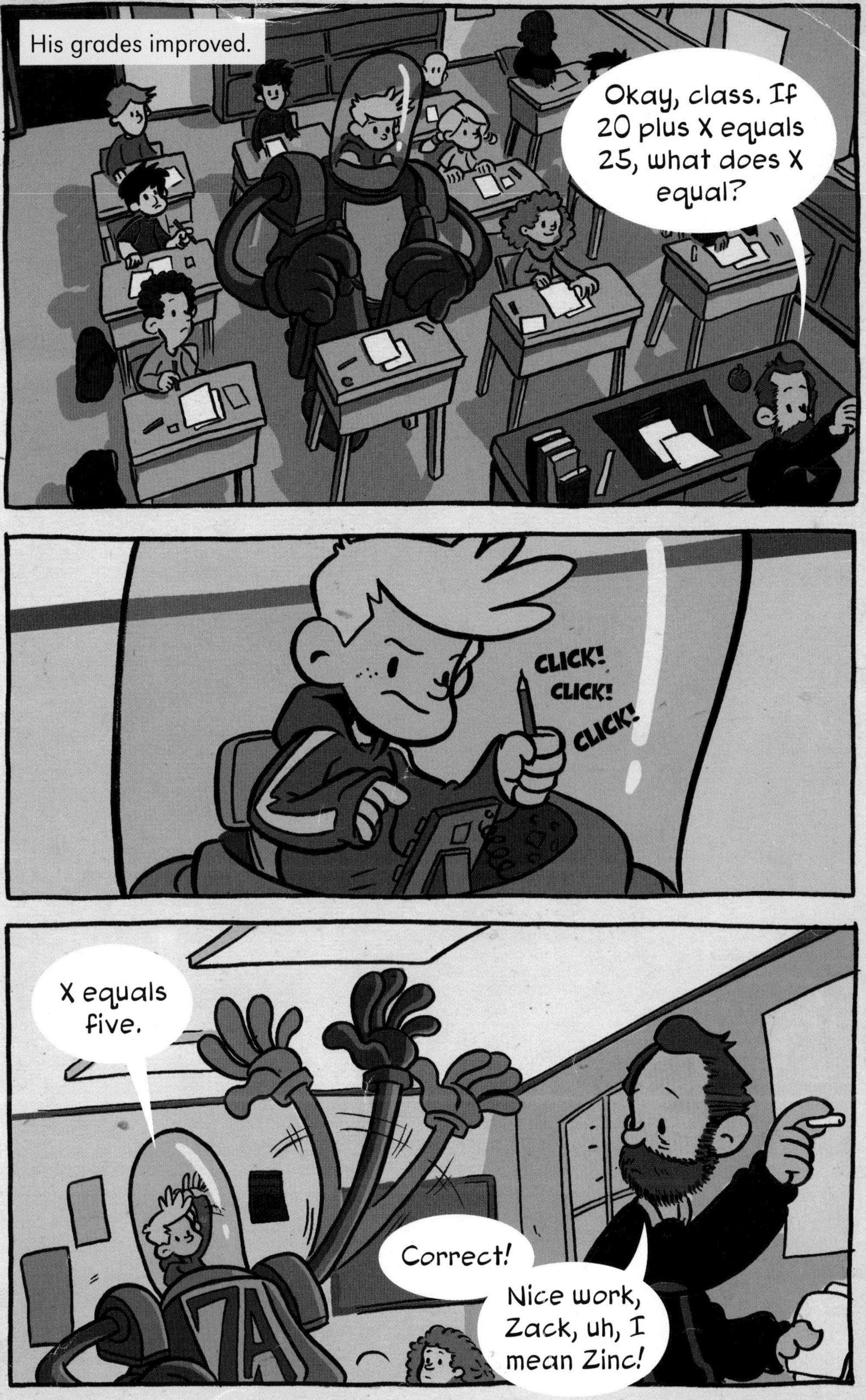

His grades improved.
Okay, class. If 20 plus X equals 25, what does X equal?
CLICK!
CLICK!
CLICK!
X equals five.
Correct!
Nice work, Zack, uh, I mean Zinc!

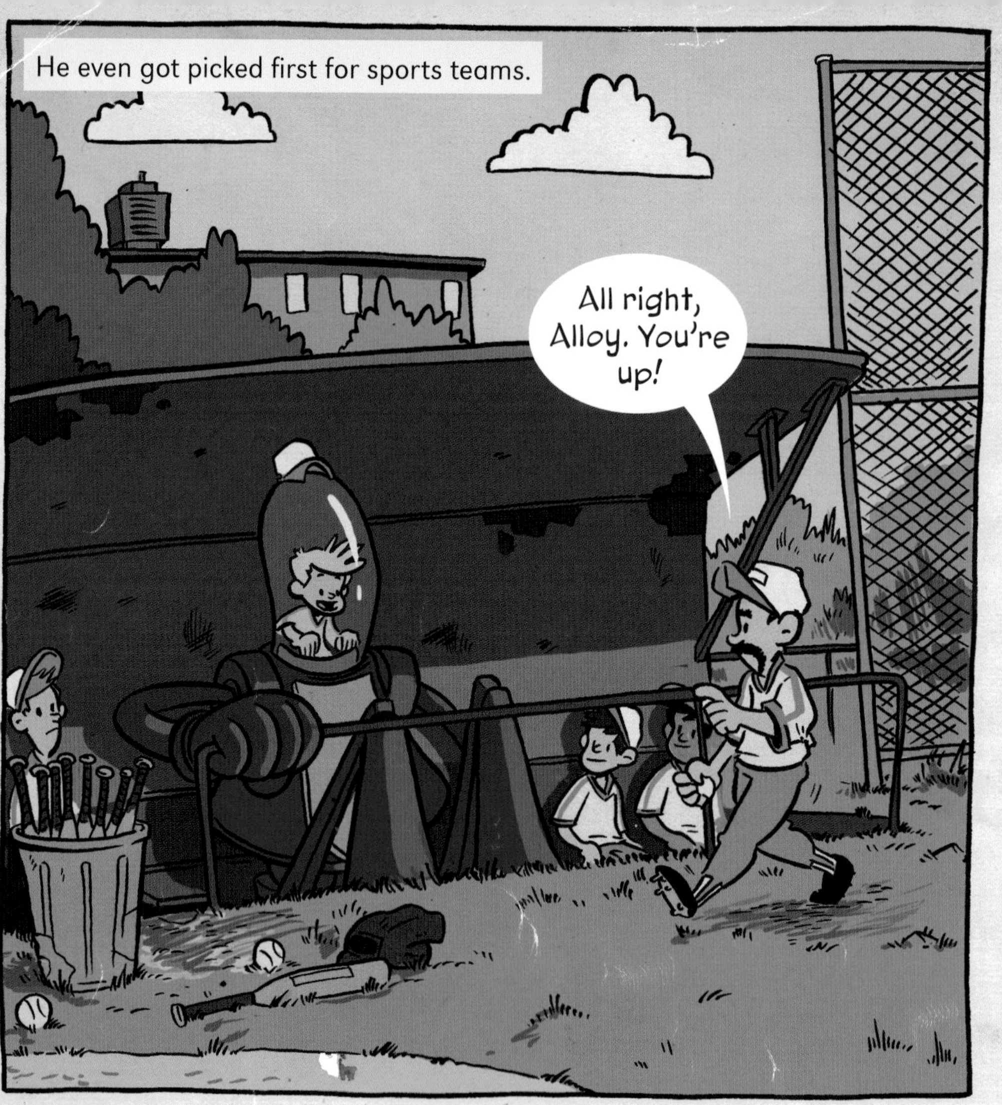
He even got picked first for sports teams.
All right, Alloy. You're up!

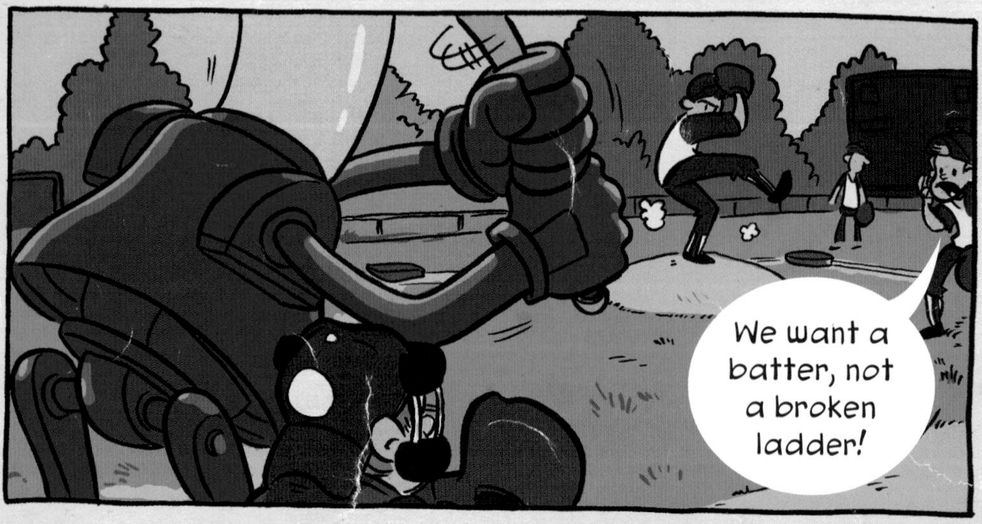
We want a batter, not a broken ladder!

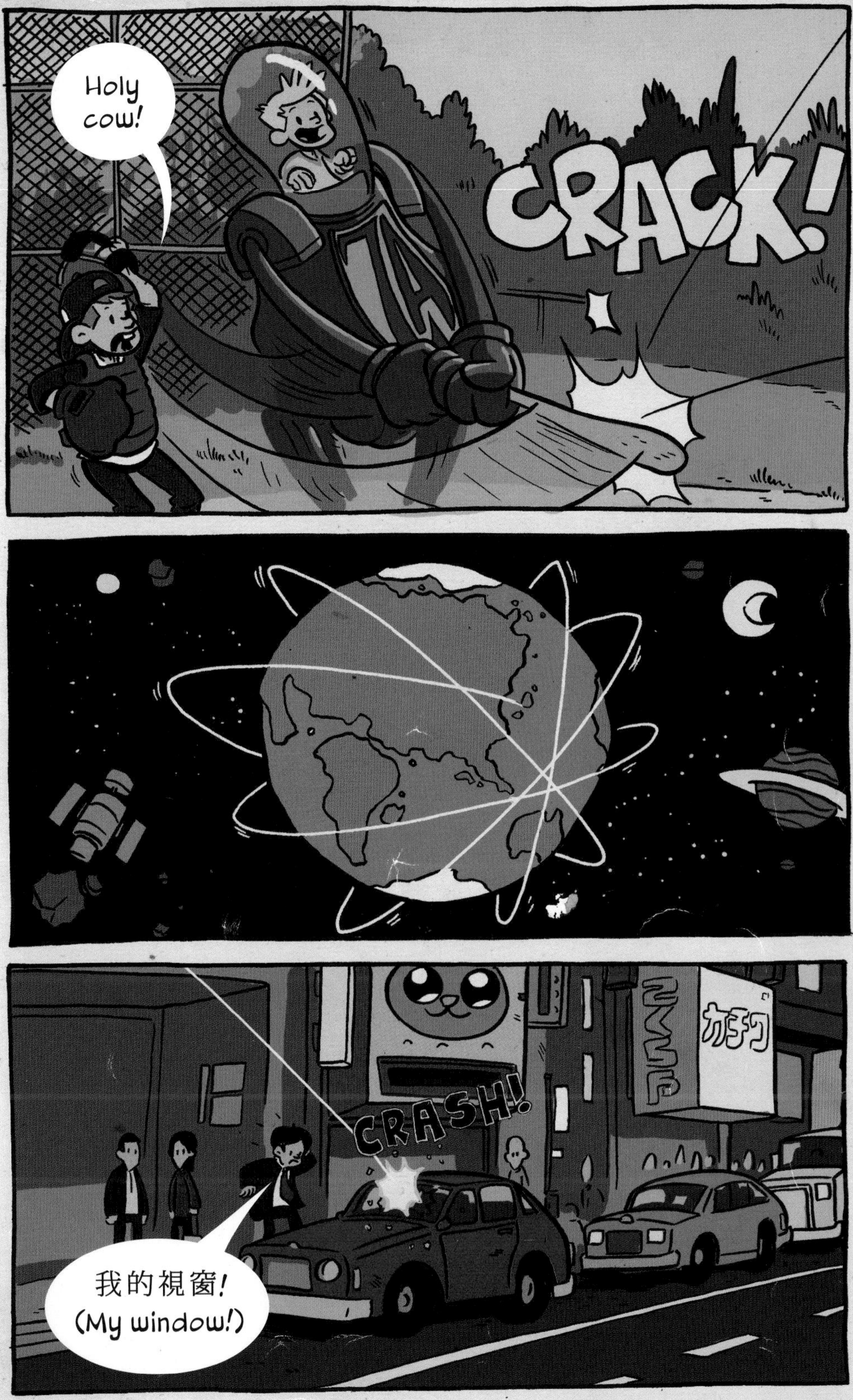
Holy cow!
CRACK!
CRASH!
我的視窗!
(My window!)

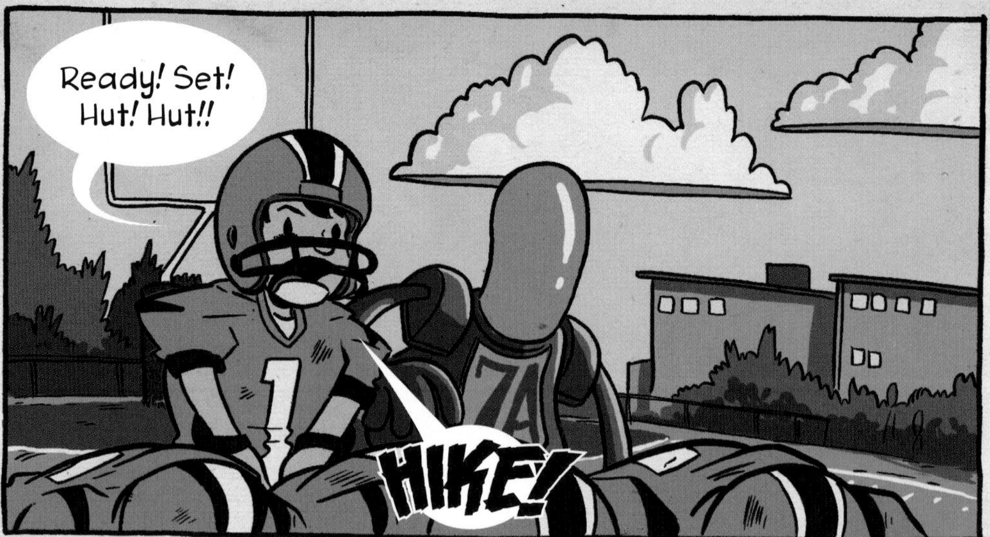
Ready! Set! Hut! Hut!!
HIKE!

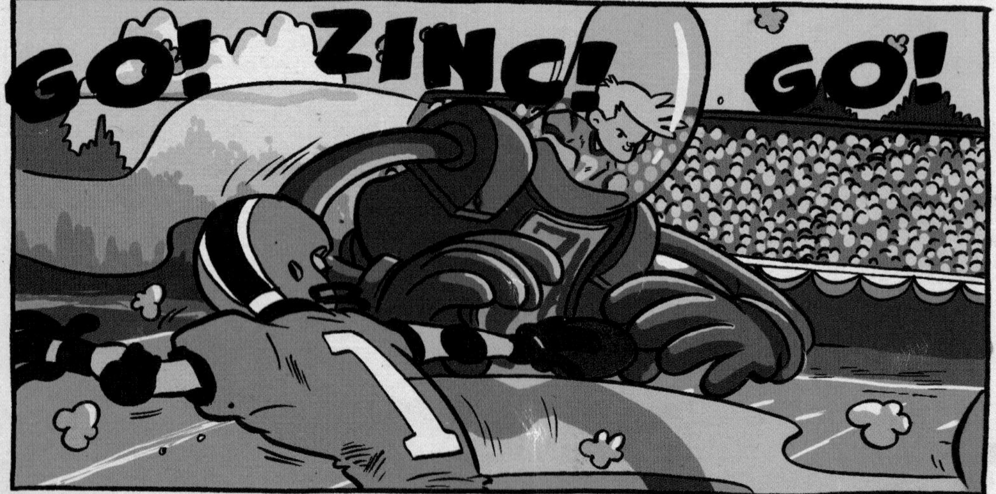
GO! ZINC! GO!

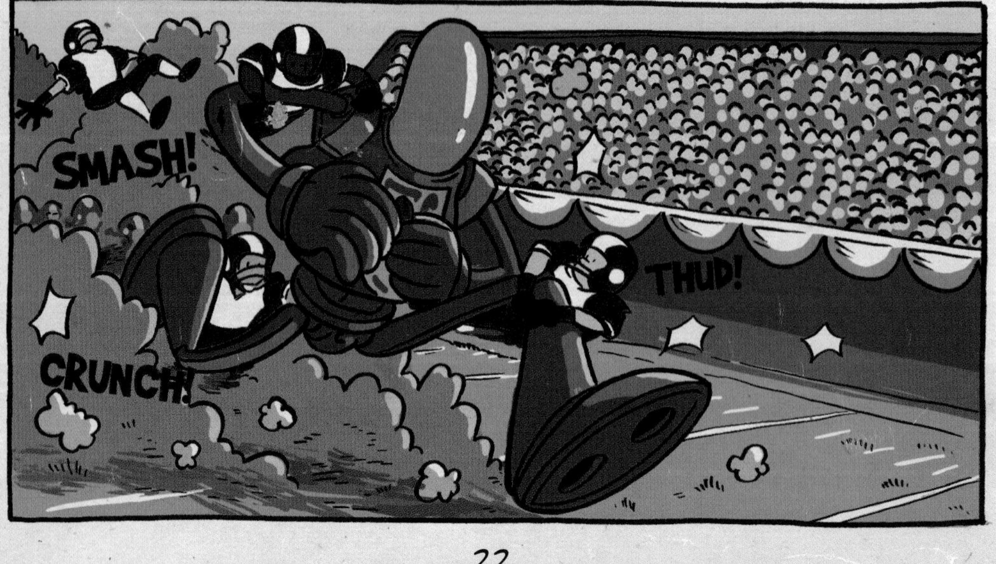
SMASH!
THUD!
CRUNCH!

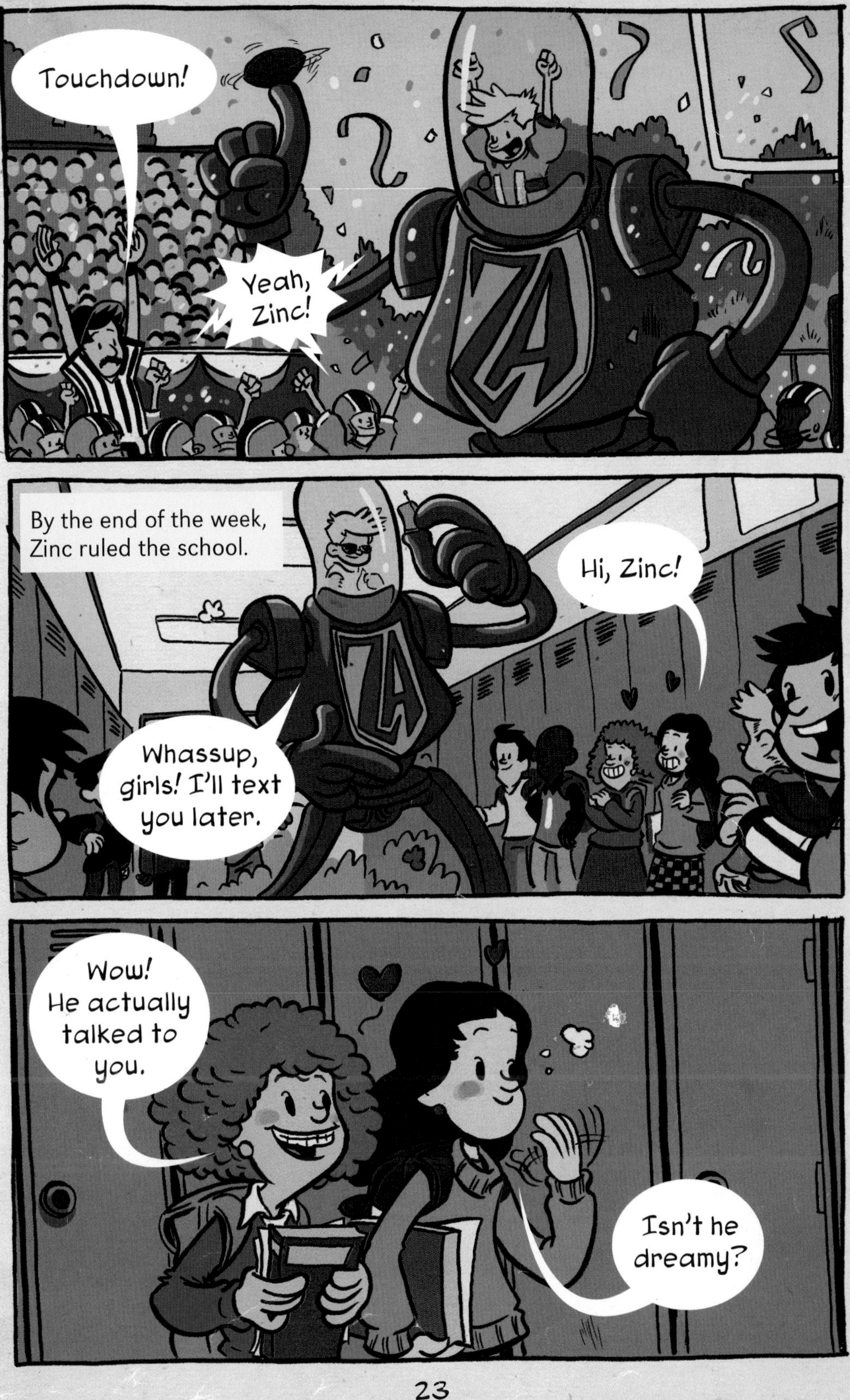
Touchdown!
Yeah, Zinc!
By the end of the week, Zinc ruled the school.
Hi, Zinc!
Whassup, girls! I'll text you later.
Wow! He actually talked to you.
Isn't he dreamy?

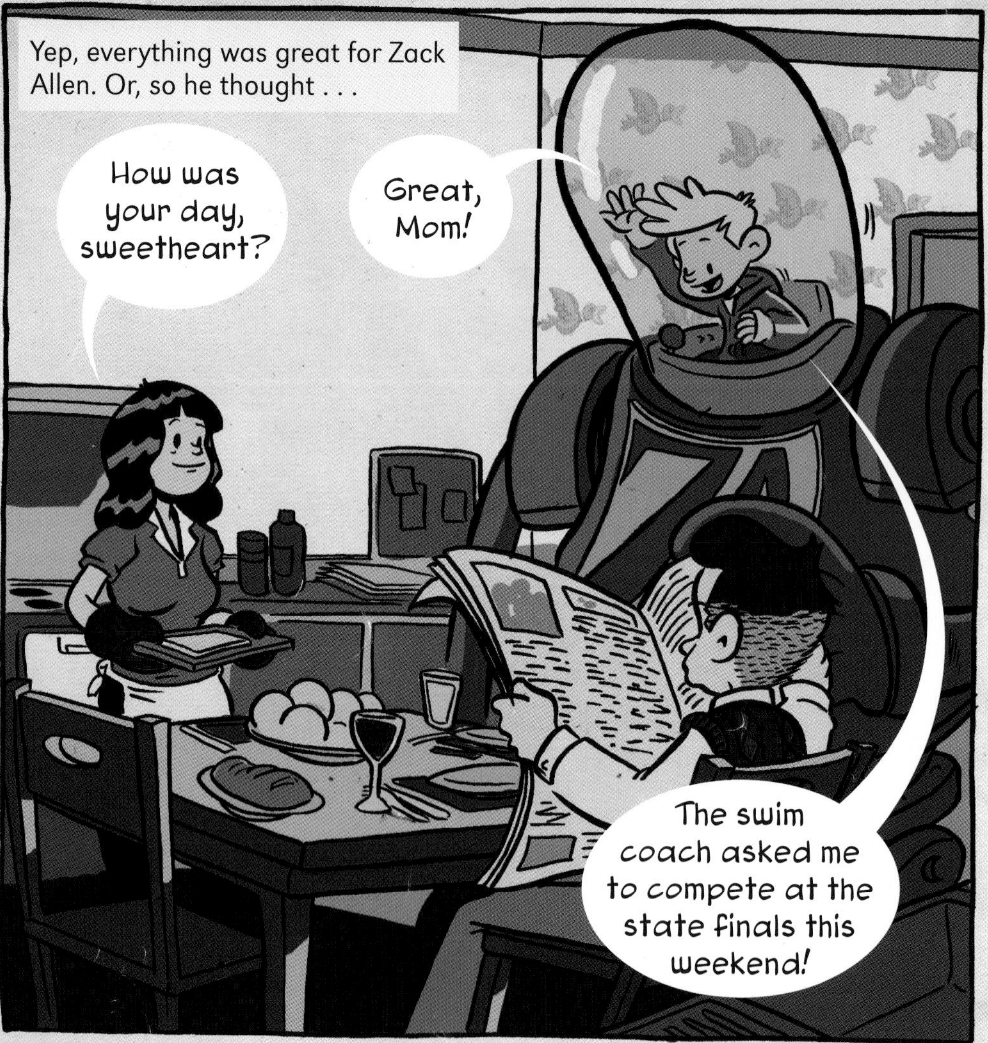
Yep, everything was great for Zack Allen. Or, so he thought . . .
How was your day, sweetheart?
Great, Mom!
The swim coach asked me to compete at the state finals this weekend!

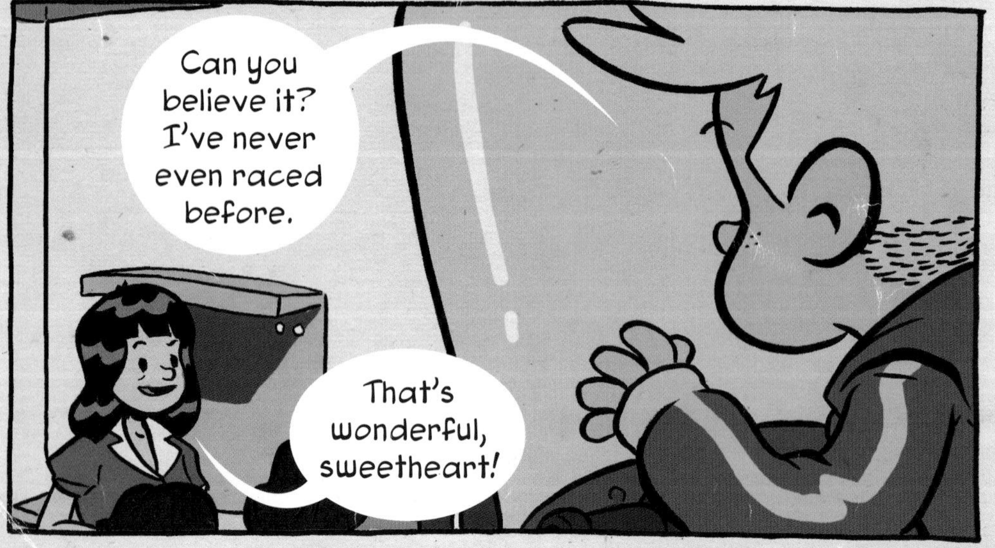
Can you believe it? I've never even raced before.
That's wonderful, sweetheart!

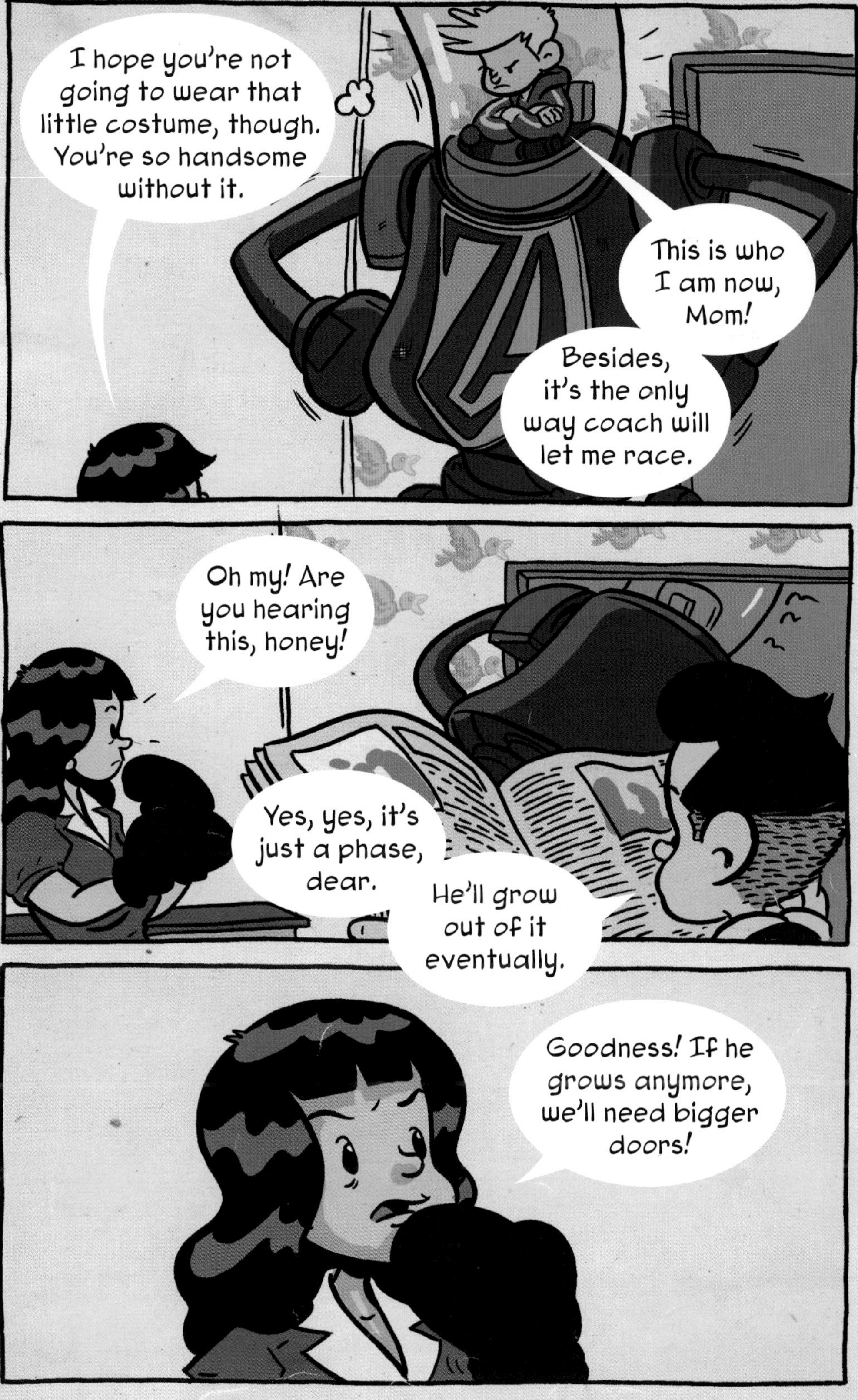
I hope you're not going to wear that little costume, though. You're so handsome without it.
This is who I am now, Mom!
Besides, it's the only way coach will let me race.
Oh my! Are you hearing this, honey!
Yes, yes, it's just a phase, dear.
He'll grow out of it eventually.
Goodness! If he grows anymore, we'll need bigger doors!

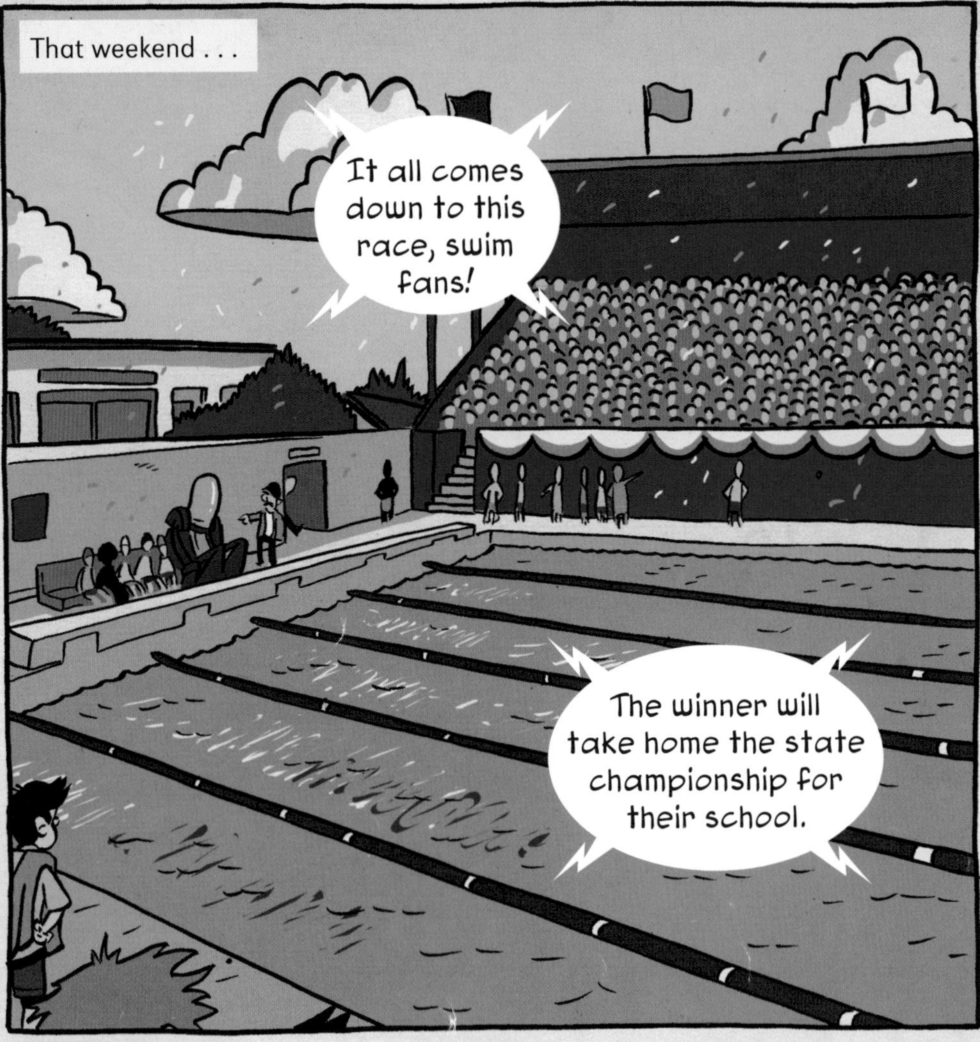
That weekend . . .
It all comes down to this race, swim fans!
The winner will take home the state championship for their school.

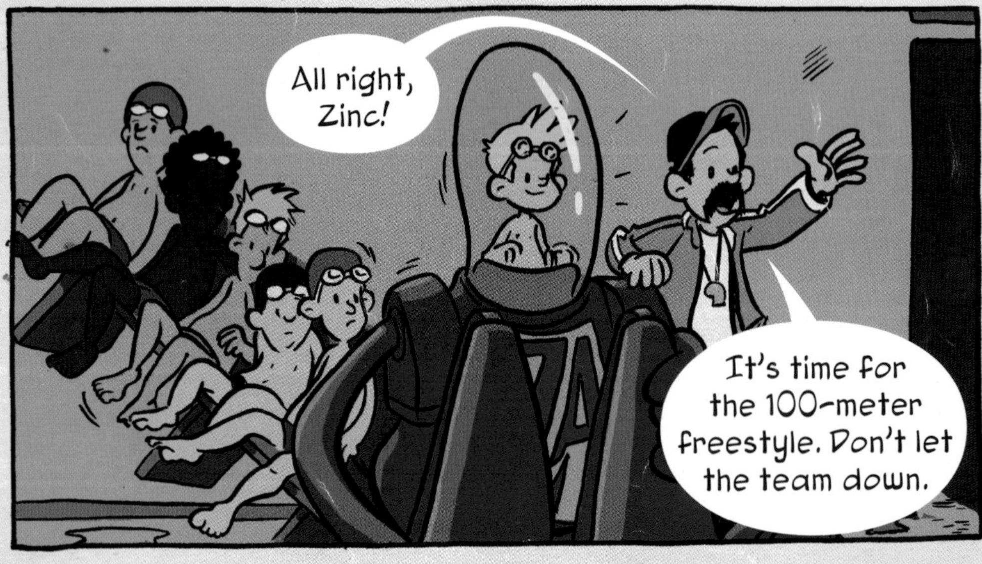
All right, Zinc!
It's time for the 100-meter freestyle. Don't let the team down.

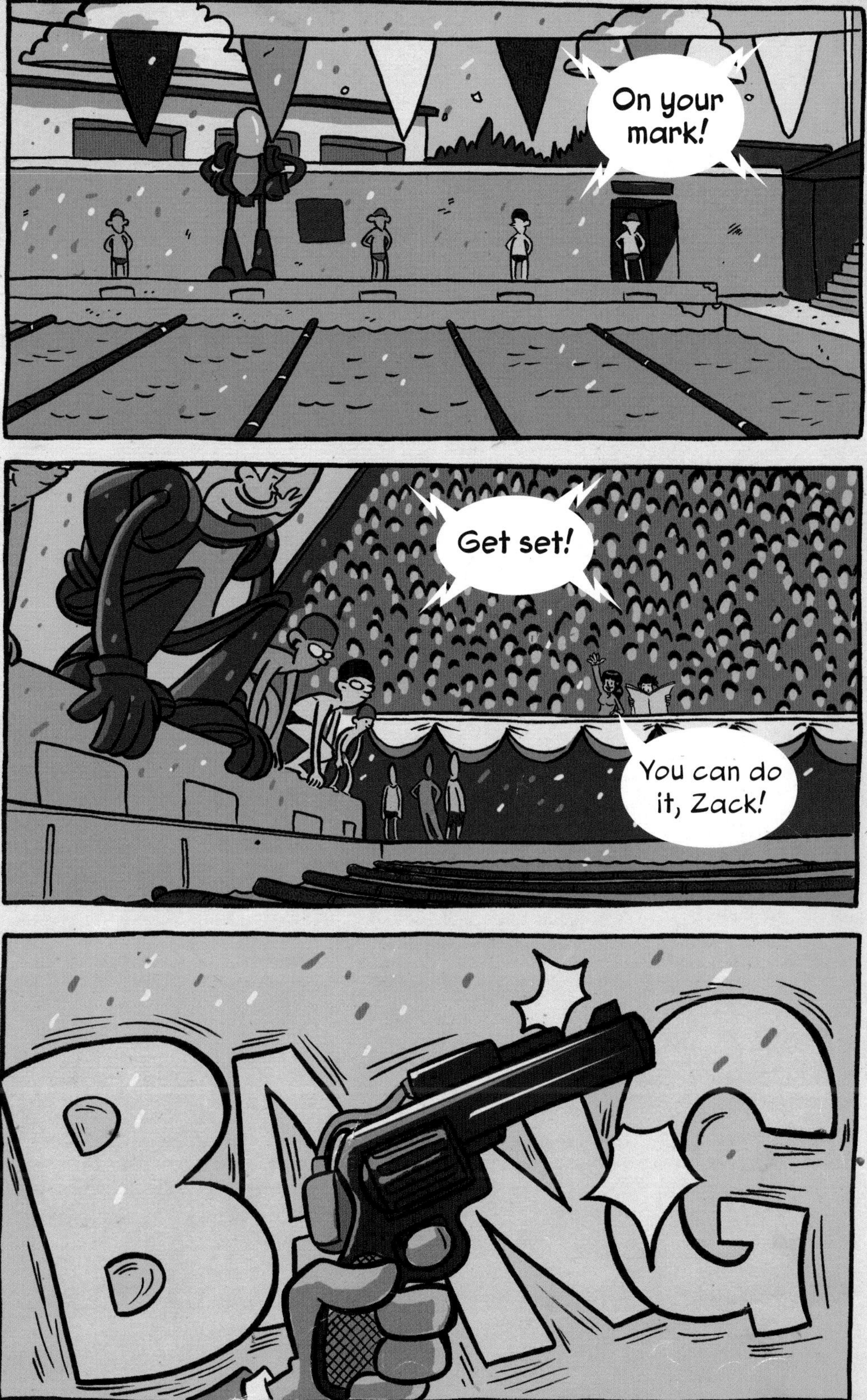
On your mark!
Get set!
You can do it, Zack!
BANG

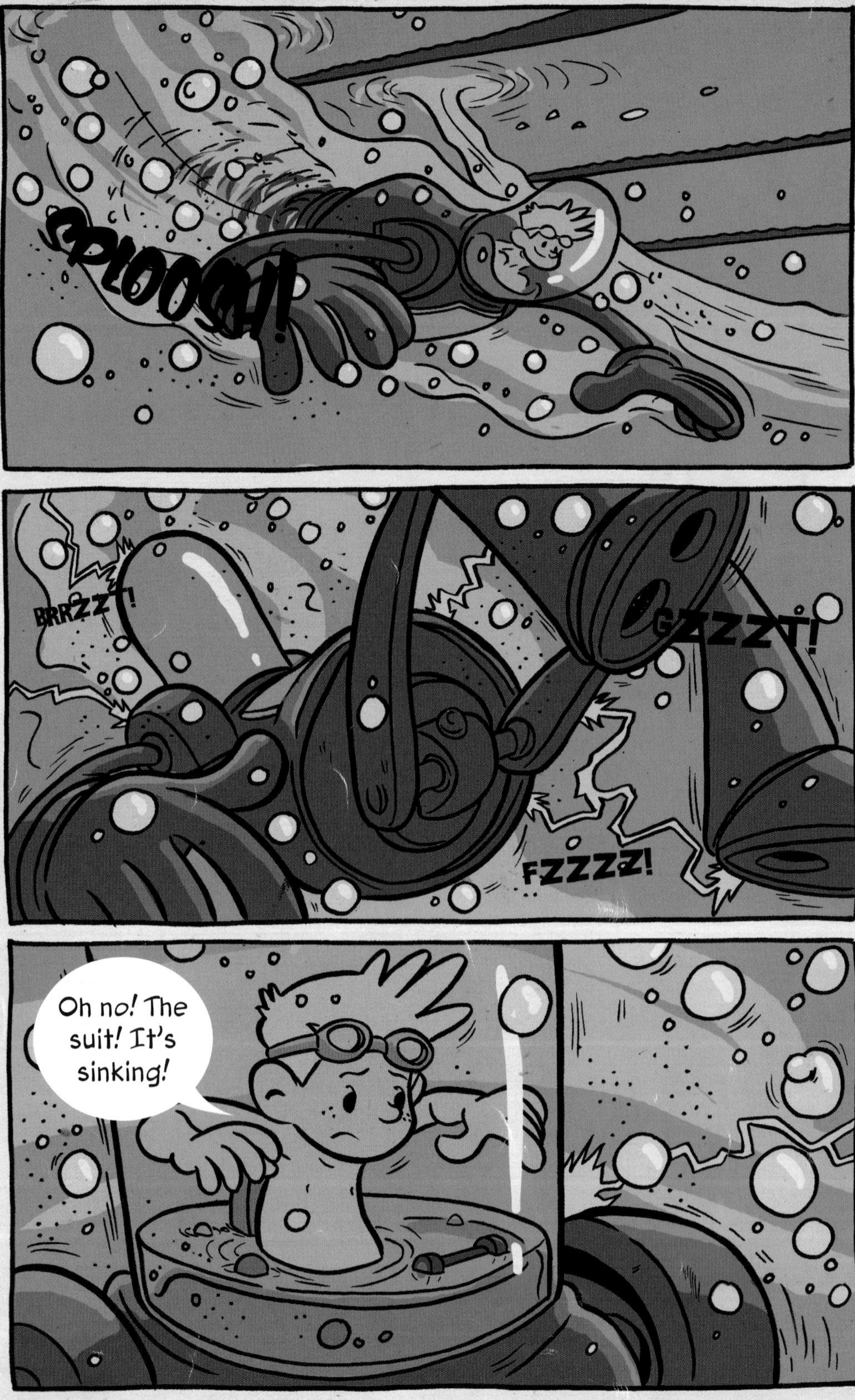
SPLOOSH!
BRRZZT!
GZZZZT!
FZZZZ!
Oh no! The suit! It's sinking!

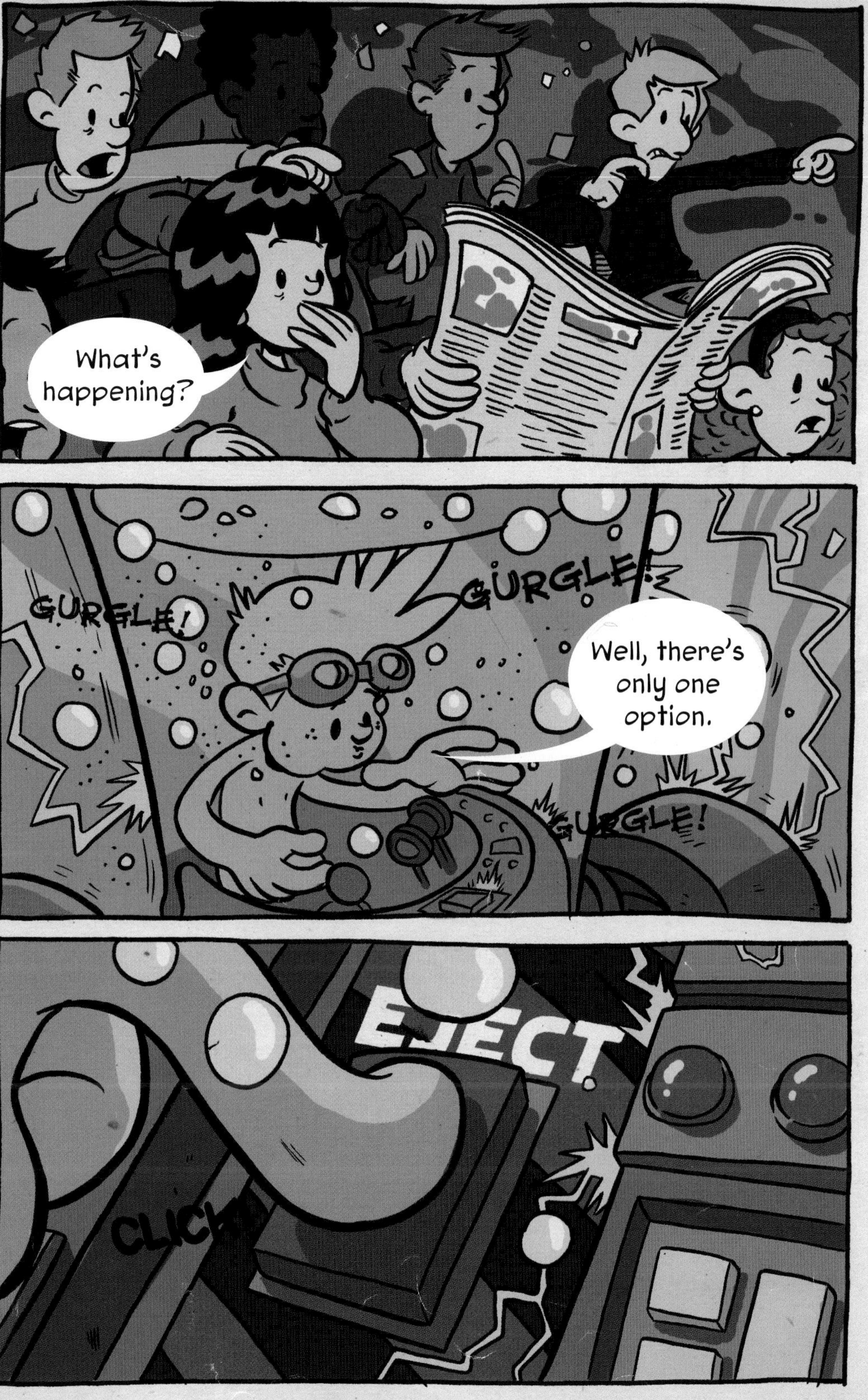
What's happening?
GURGLE!
GURGLE!
Well, there's only one option.
GURGLE!
EJECT
CLICK

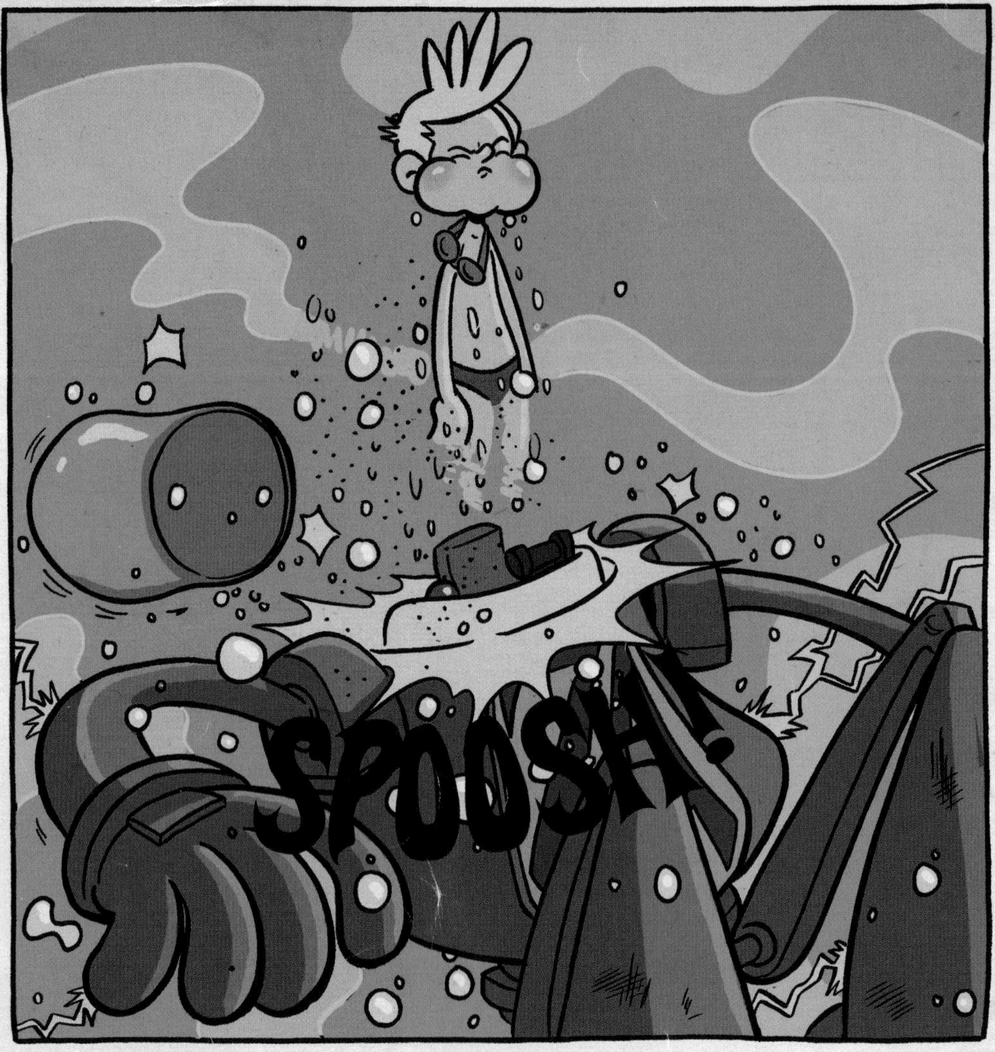
SPOOSH!

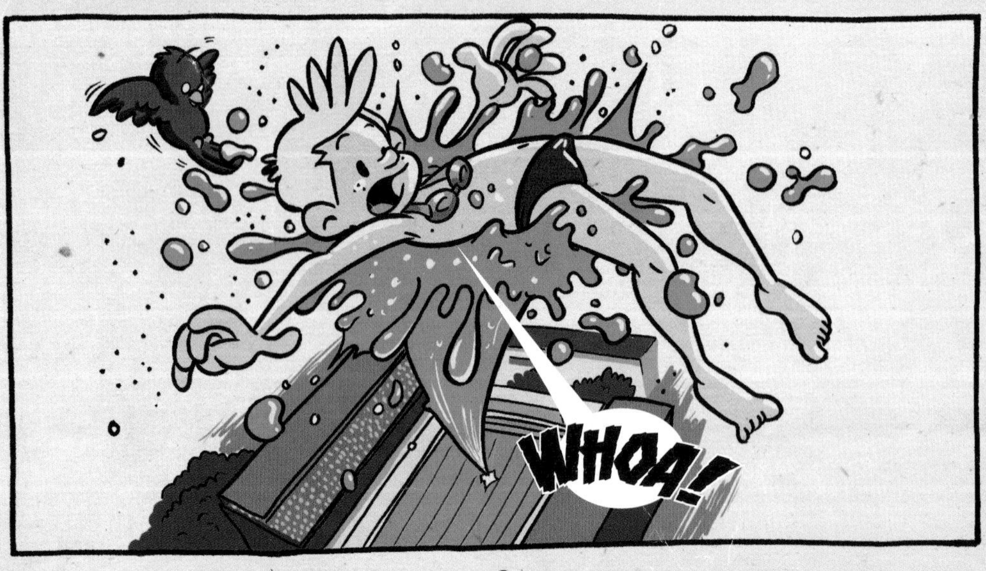
WHOA!

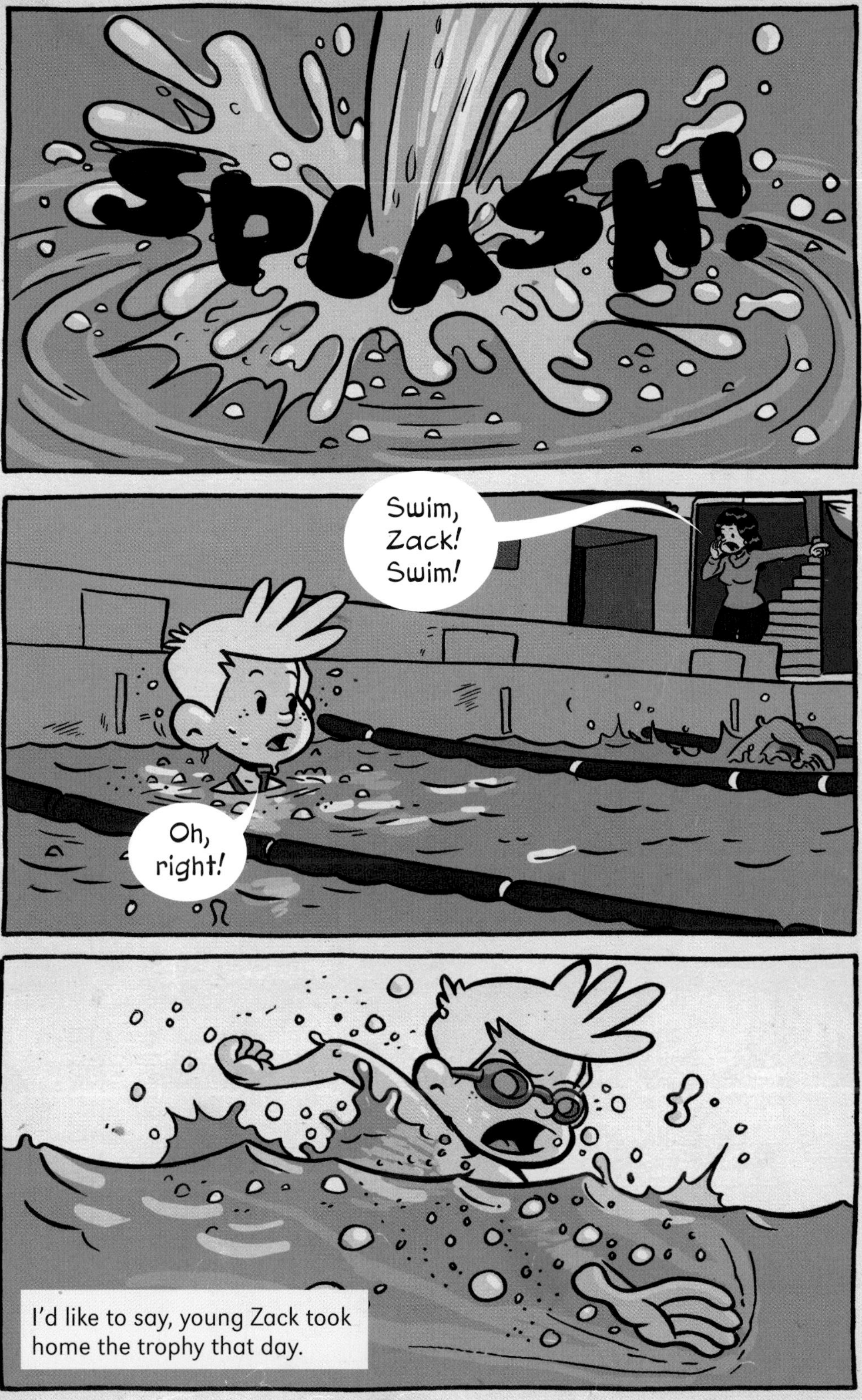
SPLASH!
Swim, Zack! Swim!
Oh, right!
I'd like to say, young Zack took home the trophy that day.

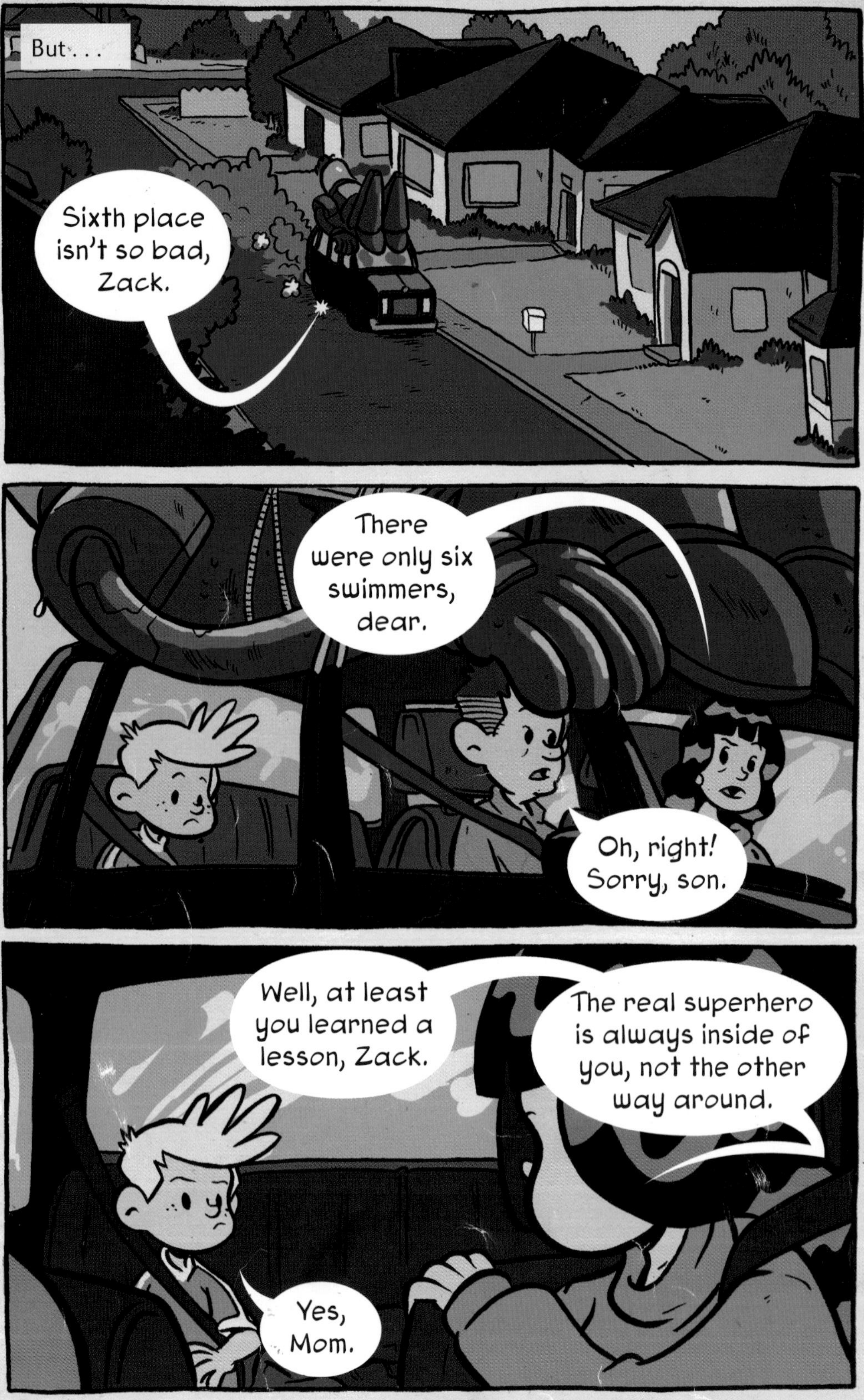
But. . .
Sixth place isn't so bad, Zack.
There were only six swimmers, dear.
Oh, right! Sorry, son.
Well, at least you learned a lesson, Zack.
The real superhero is always inside of you, not the other way around.
Yes, Mom.

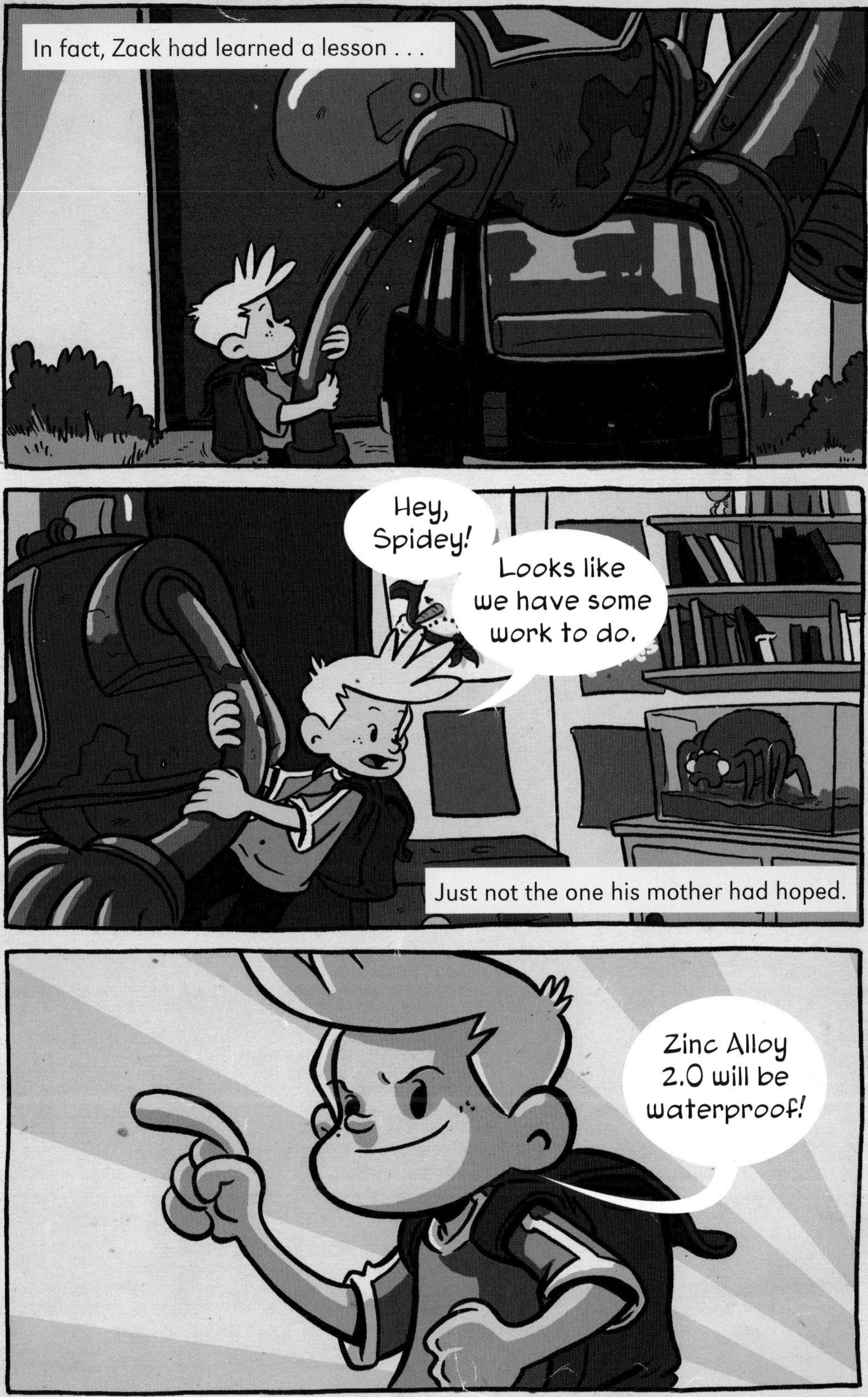
In fact, Zack had learned a lesson . . .
Hey, Spidey!
Looks like we have some work to do.
Just not the one his mother had hoped.
Zinc Alloy 2.0 will be waterproof!

# About the Author

Growing up in a small Minnesota town, Donald Lemke kept himself busy reading anything from comic books to classic novels. Today, Lemke works as a children's book editor and pursues a master's degree in publishing from Hamline University in St. Paul, Minnesota. Lemke has written a variety of children's books and graphic novels. His ideas often come to him while running along the inspiring trails near his home.

# About the Illustrator

Douglas Holgate is a freelance illustrator from Melbourne, Australia. His work has been published all around the world by Random House, Simon and Schuster, *The New Yorker* magazine, and Image Comics. His award-winning comic "Laika" appears in the acclaimed comic collection *Flight, Volume Two*.

# Glossary

**alloy** (AL-oi)—a mixture of two or more types of metal

**cafeteria** (kaf-uh-TEER-ee-uh)—the place where students are served food, or some type of mystery meat

**championship** (CHAM-pee-uhn-ship)—the contest or final game that decides the overall winner

**costume** (KOSS-toom)—clothes or an outfit worn by a person who is trying to disguise their appearance

**freestyle** (FREE-stile)—a swimming competition in which the swimmer may use any stroke

**handsome** (HAN-suhm)—attractive or good-looking

**phase** (FAZE)—a stage in someone's growth and development as a person

**waterproof** (WAW-tur-proof)—able to keep water out

**zinc** (ZINGK)—a blue-white metal used in many alloys. Iron and steel are often coated with zinc to keep them from rusting.

# More About SPORTS RECORDS

Zinc Alloy can slug a baseball all the way around the world. Here are a few sports records that even a superhero would find hard to break.

On March 2, 1962, Wilt Chamberlain of the Philadelphia Warriors set the National Basketball Association's single-game scoring record. In a game versus the New York Knicks, Chamberlain scored 100 points!

Major League Baseball's Cal Ripkin Jr. earned his superhero nickname "Iron Man." From 1982 to 1998, Ripken played 2,632 games in a row. Many believe this streak will never be broken.

Is there such a thing as the perfect athlete? Heavyweight boxer Rocky Marciano (1923–1969) comes close. During his pro career, Marciano never lost a fight, winning all of his 49 bouts.

Why is former National Hockey League player Wayne Gretzky known as the "Great One?" During his career, Gretzky scored 2,857 points. That's an incredible 894 goals and 1,963 assists.

Some records are more painful than others. While playing for the Montreal Expos in 1971, Ron Hunt was hit by a season record 50 pitches. Ouch!

Who is the fastest human on Earth? Well, that depends. Sprinter Asafa Powell holds the record for the fastest 100 meter race at 9.74 seconds. Paula Radcliffe ran the world's fastest woman's marathon (26.2 miles) in 2 hours, 17 minutes, and 18 seconds. Speedy baseball player Rickey Henderson has a record 1,406 stolen bases.

At the 1972 Summer Olympic Games, swimmer Michael Spitz won seven gold medals. That's the most gold medals by a single athlete during any Olympic Games.

Did you know only one National Football League team has ever played a perfect season? In 1972, the Miami Dolphins beat the Washington Redskins in Super Bowl VII. They ended their season with 17 wins and zero losses.

# Discussion Questions

1. Do you think Zack Allen should have been able to use the Zinc Alloy suit for sports? Was it fair to the competition? Explain your answers.

2. Why do you think Zack chose to reveal his secret identity as Zinc Alloy? What effect did this decision have on Zack's life? Use examples from the story to explain your answers.

3. Do you think Zack will continue wearing the Zinc Alloy suit to school? If he doesn't, do you think he'll still be popular? Explain.

# Writing Prompts

1. Write about the most exciting sports event you ever played in or watched. Who won the game? What made the event so fun?

2. At the end of the book, Zack Allen says he's going to make a new and improved Zinc Alloy suit. Write a story about Zinc Alloy's next adventure. What will he do? Who will he save?

3. Many comic books are written and illustrated by two different people. Write a story, and then give it to a friend to illustrate.

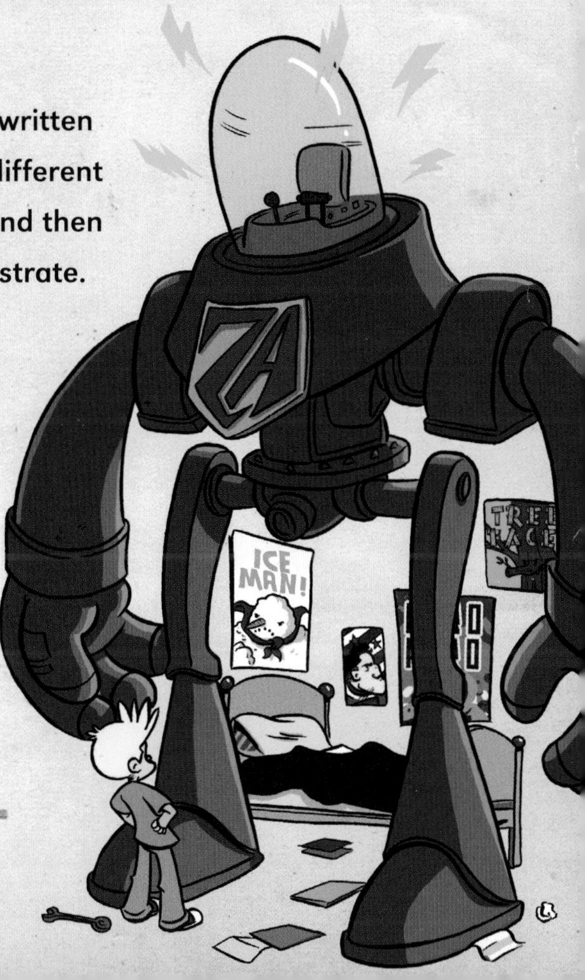
ICE MAN!

# Internet Sites

The book may be over, but the adventure is just beginning.

Do you want to read more about the subjects or ideas in this book? Want to play cool games or watch videos about the authors who write these books? Then go to FactHound. At *www.facthound.com*, you'll be able to do all that, and more. The FactHound website can also send you to other safe Internet sites.

**Check it out!**

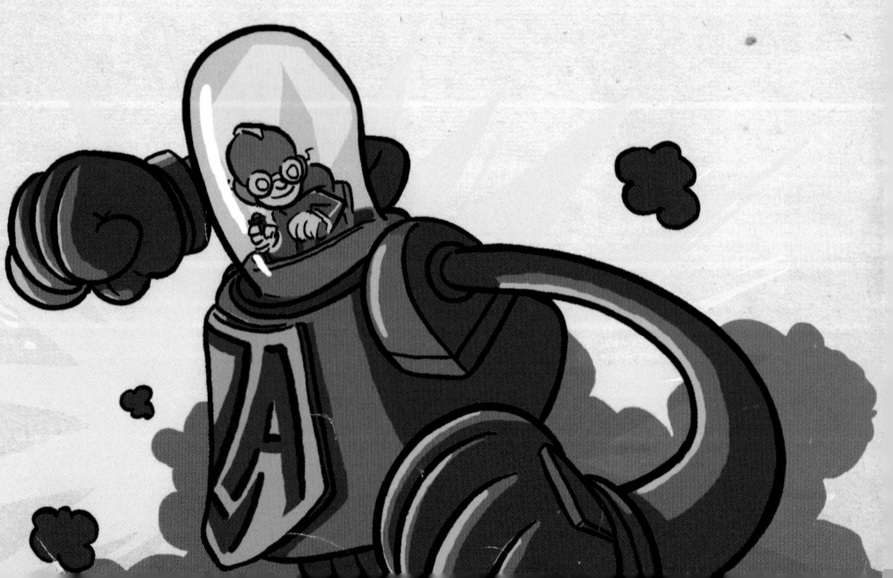

A